Bonnie Jo, Go Home

by Jeannette Eyerly

Bonnie Jo,
Go Home

Jeannette Eyerly

J. B. LIPPINCOTT COMPANY   PHILADELPHIA AND NEW YORK

The characters in this book are fictitious, and any resemblance they may bear to persons living or dead is purely coincidental.

U.S. Library of Congress Cataloging in Publication Data

Eyerly, Jeannette.
  Bonnie Jo, go home.

  SUMMARY: Despite various obstacles, a Midwestern teenager gets an abortion in New York.
  [1. Abortion—Fiction] I. Title.
PZ7.E97Bo   [Fic]   72-1863
ISBN-0-397-31390-X

For Janice

Contents

Bonnie Jo, Go Home

1 / Destination, New York

The year before, when Gloria Pardekooper dropped out of school three months before graduation and went to stay with her aunt in Omaha, everybody knew the reason why.

Later the word got back that Gloria, without ever seeing the baby, had given it up for adoption and was working as a salad girl at the new Holiday Inn.

Things weren't going to happen like that, however, for Bonnie Jo Jackson. She wasn't going to have her baby.

Instead, she was going to New York and have an abortion. Each time she had to force herself to say, or even think, the word. But she had to get used to it. After all, there wasn't anything wrong with having one. In New York, an abortion was a perfectly legal operation. In lots of other places, too, Colorado and California, for instance. If it weren't for a stupid hundred-year-old law where *she* lived, she could have it right there in Cedar City.

Beneath shuttered lashes, she glanced at her father. His jaw was set and his hands were holding the steering wheel of the car so tightly it made his knuckles look white. He'd scarcely said a word since he'd picked her up in front of her stepfather's house. But that was all right. Already, there'd been too much talk, too many threats, and too many tears. All she wanted now was to get it over with and come back home again.

Under different circumstances, New York would be exciting. But in the spring, there wasn't a prettier place in the world than Cedar City. Buds were showing pink in the flowering crabs planted along the parkway. Redbud trees were in bloom. The forsythia all over town was so goldenly profuse it dazzled the eye.

It was even nicer when it was early, like this, and there wasn't so much traffic. In most of the houses people were still sleeping.

She herself had hardly slept at all. She'd set the alarm for five o'clock, but there would have been no need to. When it was time for it to go off, she'd been lying wide awake beneath the covers for hours.

Because she'd taken a bath the night before, now all she had to do was dress. Shivering, she peeled off her nightgown and looked at herself sidewise in the mirror above her bureau. She didn't show at all. Not likely, the doctor said at eight weeks, but still . . . She was glad she didn't show. It would have made it worse somehow if she did.

She folded the nightgown she'd taken off and put it into her little suitcase. She probably wouldn't need it. With any luck, she'd be home that night. But in case something should go wrong—if the plane should be late and make her miss her appointment at the clinic at two o'clock that afternoon and she had to stay overnight—she would have clean underwear and a comb and toothbrush with her.

The room was chilly and she dressed quickly. Bra, panties, a cotton knit dress with narrow stripes of navy blue and kelly green going round and round. And her new sandals. She had got them at Burt's and they'd cost $7.95 and they had all kinds of straps and buckles and nail-head trim. She was proud of her feet which were very narrow and as soft and white as her hands. Although none of the girls she knew wore nail polish on their toes, she did. It was called Princess Pink. Thirty-nine cents in the small size, at Woolworth's.

In the bathroom, she washed her face and brushed her teeth then put on lipstick. She never used very much, but today, even the little did not seem right, and she took it off.

Back in her room, she snapped shut her suitcase and looked into her purse for about the tenth time to see that her airplane ticket and billfold were still there. She started for the door, then remembering her poncho —it was the only wrap she was taking—went back and got it. Lena, who'd married her father soon after the divorce and knitted while she watched the daytime serials and quiz shows, had made it for her. It was striped in a lot of different shades of blue and had long fringe.

Bonnie Jo was surprised to see her mother standing at the head of the stairs. Her mother had said she wouldn't get up to say good-bye because Merle, Bonnie's stepfather, wouldn't like it, but in any case, there she was. Her hair, which was as blond as Bonnie's own, but not natural, was hanging down around her face—

Merle wouldn't let her go to bed in rollers—and she looked as if she hadn't slept much either. She'd cried sometime during the night and tears had smudged some leftover mascara.

She put her arms around Bonnie Jo, kissed her, and without saying a word scurried, like the White Rabbit going down the rabbit hole, into her bedroom where Merle quite audibly still slept. He didn't like to wake up and not find her there.

Her stepsister, Precious, who was four and a half and slept in the bedroom next to hers, made no sound at all.

A dickcissel, facing into the rising sun, said his name, "Dick sis, sis, sssss," over and over again.

"I guess we're going to be in plenty of time," her father said, "Your plane doesn't leave until seven ten and it's still not quite six thirty."

Even so, hundreds of cars were already parked in the metered lot. Bonnie Jo tried to think about all the people it took to run an airport; about all the other people who would be taking the same plane she did to Chicago; about those who would be changing at O'Hare for New York. But it wasn't any use.

All she could think about was Mark. The last time she'd been at the airport, they were together. They were going steady then and just to ride around, just to be with him, was enough. They'd parked in the metered lot to watch the planes come in. Because the motor was running, they had the windows down a bit.

Mark was careful about everything. When a cop in a patrol car had come up and shone his big flashlight in on them, they had laughed because they weren't doing anything. Not even holding hands.

The cop, who was young, had laughed, too, then driven on.

Now, she stifled a sudden little sob for all she'd lost and would never have again.

Inside the airport building, her father, who had been propelling her forward, stopped suddenly. "You don't have to go, you know. It's not too late to change your mind."

The two of them stood like an island while waves of early morning travelers swirled around them.

She raised her eyes to his face. He'd not shaved. She'd not really looked at him at all that morning, until then. Because he was fair, like she was, his whiskers didn't show too much. It was the clean shirt and the carefully tied tie which made the shabby suit look shabbier, that destroyed her.

For the one hundred and eighty dollars the plane ticket had cost, he could have bought all kinds of new clothes. The two hundred dollars in traveler's checks—a hundred dollars for the doctor at the clinic and another hundred for any miscellaneous expenses she might have—that she carried in her fringed leather shoulder bag would have made the down payment on a new car. Although none of it—losing his job with Fairchild and Company or the divorce from her mother just three years ago—was really his fault, it was too late now to feel sorry for him. All the sorriness she had room for was contained within herself.

He looked at his watch. "You could still get to school on time."

Before she could answer, the flight was called. The voice was rich, disembodied. It might have come from God. ". . . Three-forty-seven, O'Hare Airport, Chicago, now boarding at Gate C 3."

As if they had been programmed, people around them started moving toward the escalator that led upward toward the boarding area.

Bonnie Jo picked up her suitcase that stood between them.

"I'll go with you to the gate," her father said.

She shook her head. "No. If you do, I'll cry."

"We don't want that," he said. He cleared his throat, again looked at his watch. "I think I'll go directly to the office. I can use the extra hour. I've kind of gotten behind the last couple of weeks."

She chose not to think of the reason for him getting behind in his work. Ever since, in her desperation, she had come to him, there had been nothing but worry.

The minute hand of the big clock on the wall was moving faster and faster.

"I guess . . . I guess I'd better go."

There were little beads of moisture on her father's upper lip. He took out his handkerchief and wiped them away. "Good-bye, then. I guess. And good luck. Though, like I said, you don't have to go. Having a baby isn't the end of the world, you know. We could work things out some way. Some other way."

Standing near them, a young couple was saying good-bye. The boy was wearing a paratrooper's uniform with some battle ribbons and the girl was crying. By her side, a baby in an airport stroller, with "Planned Parenthood" stamped across the canvas back, stared off into the middle distance as he sucked his pacifier.

Bonnie Jo looked away. "I have to go."

"Well, then, good-bye again," her father said. "If I don't hear from you to the contrary, I'll meet the plane that gets in from Chicago at eleven twenty tonight. If something happens, I mean, if you don't get—you know, well . . . through, you call me. And go to the YW. The YW is the best place for a young girl to stay in New York City."

"O.K.," she said. "All right. Don't worry."

Now, all she wanted was to be on her way. If he didn't leave, if he didn't stop talking, she thought she might scream. It was too much that her father, who was the one who didn't *want* her to have it, had given her the money, while her mother and Merle, who thought it was such a great idea, hadn't given her a cent.

He leaned forward to kiss her but she pulled away so his lips only brushed her cheek. Turning, and walking fast, she followed a fat woman wearing a purple pants suit and clogs toward the escalator.

If it had not been for the woman in the purple pants suit, she would have been all right. But her friend, Iris Beason, who was the only one at school who knew, had told her if she couldn't get a seat next to a window to get one on the aisle. Anything was better, Iris said—she had flown to California twice on TWA and knew from experience—than being trapped in the middle of one of those sections with three seats in a row.

But the one empty seat on the aisle was next to the woman in the purple pants suit and she took it.

A baby could have fastened the seat belt but Purple Pants Suit leaned over and did it for her. "There? All tucked in as snug as a bug in a rug?"

Bonnie Jo forced herself to smile and say thank you. She did not want to talk. She wanted to look around. An elderly couple was tottering down the aisle. Behind them, a pretty girl with dark, shoulder-length hair; next, the young paratrooper she'd seen saying good-bye to his wife.

"Your first flight?"

Purple Pants Suit answered the question before Bonnie could reply. "Right! I always can tell. Nervousness shows. Little things. Like the way you're twisting the fringe on your poncho. That sort of white look around your mouth. I noticed it, first thing." She put a fat-fingered hand with many rings on Bonnie's knee. "Well, don't worry. Nothing is going to happen. Unless we're hijacked, and that's a different story. Or like somebody having a bomb aboard. But except for that, the pilot of this plane knows the way from here to Chicago like you know the way from your house to school."

A muffled roar seemed to come from all around them and the plane began to vibrate. A few minutes later it began to move down the runway. Bonnie closed her eyes. When the plane left the ground, her stomach seemed to rise up to meet it.

When she opened her eyes, all she could see across the bulk of her companion was a vaporous white mass outside the window. One of the stewardesses was explaining about oxygen masks that would drop from the ceiling right over everybody's head if something went wrong. Another stewardess had started moving down the aisle with a pile of magazines.

Bonnie Jo did not take one. She had her own. Her friend, Iris Beason, had given it to her at school the day before as a sort of going-away present. It was called *Romantic Love.* All the stories in it were true.

"Oh, you young girls and romance!" The woman in the purple pants suit had leaned over to read the title, was laughing indulgently. "I remember when that was all I thought of—morning, noon and night. Love and romance.

"Your boyfriend meeting you in Chicago?"

Almost imperceptibly, Bonnie Jo shook her head and began reading. Less than ten minutes later, however, the woman beside her was at it again.

"Your boyfriend meeting you in *New York?*"

A full-page photograph of a girl who looked, Bonnie Jo thought, a little like she did, stared back at her from the magazine. The caption beneath it read, "Not until I met Hilary did I learn that love and sex were not the same."

"I haven't a boyfriend, really," she said.

"Have it your way," the woman spoke tolerantly. "Though I don't believe for a minute that a girl as pretty as you are—though you could stand a little fattening—hasn't got a boyfriend. That blond hair of yours is real. I know that without asking. I worked as a beauty operator for two years before I married my husband. After we were married, though, and the babies started coming, I gave it up. You can't serve God and mammal, as my mother used to say."

"Mammon." Although Bonnie Jo spoke timidly, she knew she was right. Miss Hartsung, who taught senior English and wanted practically everybody to go to college—even her—had quoted some lines from *Paradise Lost* to class one day. It was funny that she remembered, because they hadn't made much sense to her then, or now. "Mammon led them on, Mammon, the least erected Spirit that fell from heav'n. . . ."

"Mammal," said Purple Pants Suit solidly. "She never went past eighth grade, but my mother should know. Even though she's almost ninety, her mind is still as clear as a bell. But that's quibbling. Mammal, or whatever you said it was. What difference does it make? What matters is *this!"* She leaned over and shook a bracelet, from which a number of silver discs were dangling, under Bonnie Jo's nose. "Kids! Grandchildren!" She began ticking off the discs like a checkout clerk at a supermarket. "Tamara, six; Bobbie, five;

22

Leona Marie, three and a half. They're my daughter Glenda's. Then there's Sharry Sue and Johnnie Fitz— they're four and seven—the twins, Lawrence Welk and Eddie Sullivan, three in June. They belong to my son Harry. He's with Shell. These four belong to my daughter, Velma, who lives in Detroit. Grace, ten, she's named after me; Thomas, eight . . ." Interrupting herself before she could finish, she looked at Bonnie Jo accusingly. "You've not been listening! You've not heard a word I said!"

"I . . . I'm afraid I don't feel very well." Even before the twin set of lights reading "Fasten Seat Belts" and "No Smoking, Please" had appeared on a panel at the front of the compartment, she'd started feeling sick. When the plane seemed to be gently rising and falling like a ship at sea, she felt even worse.

The woman in the purple pants suit gave her a sharp, investigation look. "If there's any chance you're going to throw up, there's a paper bag to throw up in in the pocket of that seat there in front of you." She pinched her nostrils and tried, unsuccessfully, to draw in some of her bulk overflowing on Bonnie Jo's seat. "Though in all my years of flying airplanes around the country to visit my children, I've never yet known anybody on an airplane to throw up unless they happened to be pregnant." She paused, repeated the word. "Pregnant, not married—not even engaged—and going to New York. . . ." She eyed Bonnie Jo sharply. "You know, I wouldn't wonder but what I know the reason.

23

I wouldn't wonder but what you're one of those girls who go to New York to get ..."

The rest of the sentence was obliterated in the sudden zooming of the plane as it lost altitude in preparation for landing. Bonnie Jo closed her eyes, but the unspoken word still hung in the air about her, endlessly repeating itself. Abortion ... abortion ... abortion ... She tried to remember a prayer to say but all she could think of was "Mammon led them on—the least erected Spirit that fell from heav'n," and that did her no good at all.

2 / A New Seat-Mate

Afterward, Bonnie Jo could not remember leaving the plane, only being moved along by other passengers. Flying had disembodied her. She felt as if she no longer belonged anywhere, heaven or earth. In the flow of other passengers, she had simply drifted until she found herself standing alone at a sort of crossroads of wide corridors somewhere inside the airport. The woman in the purple pants suit, who just by looking at her could tell, had disappeared. The young soldier, whose wife and baby had been left behind, likewise had vanished, as had the elderly couple and the pretty girl with the shoulder-length black hair.

Still, there were plenty of people. Uniformed stewardesses, carrying small neat suitcases, walked briskly by in their twinkling patent leather pumps. Mothers with babies in strollers; mothers with babies in arms; mothers with babies, papoose-style, on their backs. There were children who either clutched at their mothers' skirts, sometimes almost too high to reach, or children who ran madly ahead with their distraught parents in pursuit.

There was no place to sit, so putting down her suitcase, she leaned against the wall until she should feel better. The hands of a clock over her head pointed to eight thirty. The plane for New York would not leave for another forty minutes, so she had plenty of time to find the gate from which it would depart. Somewhere, nearby, there would be one of those television screens—they were everywhere, her friend Iris had explained—that would tell her where to go.

She still did not feel well. Not as bad as she had felt on the plane. But still squeamish. Getting that sick feeling in the morning as soon as she got up was what made her think she might be pregnant. If she had regular periods like Iris, she would have known. People like Iris were lucky. Every twenty-eight days, just like that, she had the curse. Iris could even tell a couple of days ahead of time because she hated everybody and didn't want Gordy Pinter, who was her boyfriend, to touch her. Not that he ever did much more, Iris said, though she wished he would. Within reason. But as Gordy was going to be a priest, it was understandable. All Iris hoped was that by the time she and Gordy could even think about getting married, the church would have shaped up and celibacy wouldn't be the rule anymore.

Iris, however, was the one who had insisted she see a doctor. His name was Dr. Jepson and she had chosen his name at random out of the yellow pages of the phone book.

Iris said Bonnie Jo dared not go to any doctor either of them knew. When Dr. Jepsen told her she was pregnant—though by then she was almost sure, herself—she thought she'd die. He thought about eight weeks, and that was what she thought, too. The first time she wasn't even sure it happened. She'd been drunk. So it had to be the second time, when she knew what she was doing. That didn't make it right, though, and in a way, even worse.

Dr. Jepson, however, though he was old and doddering and had come out of the Yellow Pages, was nice. He'd given her some pills to take, free samples that he had on hand, to help the morning sickness and a lot of pamphlets about prenatal care and the joys of approaching motherhood. He'd been full of advice, too, about going straight to her parents and telling them everything. They would understand. They would help her. What a laugh that had been. Telling Iris what he'd said, she laughed until she cried. Then she got so hysterical that Iris had to slap her to make her stop.

The hands of the clock over her head had been moving steadily on as she stood there. It was now eight fifty. In twenty minutes the plane for New York would be leaving. She picked up her suitcase and on impulse moved down the corridor that ran at right angles to the place she'd been standing. She passed a door with a sign on it reading "Women," but did not go in though she would have liked to. A little further on, she saw one of the television screens Iris had told her about. She stopped and without putting down her suitcase tried to read the flickering type. As she watched, one line of type at the top vanished and another line appeared at the bottom. Nowhere did she see Flight 687 for New York. Flight 687.

Her heart was pounding. A man with a small, neat beard and wearing a beret, who had been standing beside her and likewise studying the screen, apparently found what he was looking for and moved on.

Though she was sure she had memorized the flight number correctly, she fumbled in her fringed bag for her ticket. Six eight seven was right after all. When she looked at the television screen again, it was the first number she saw. Gate A 11. It had been there all the time!

But Gate A 11 could be anywhere. It could be the direction from which she'd come, or in either of the two corridors that forked off from it in a giant Y.

She could feel little beads of perspiration forming at her hairline and on her upper lip.

"Ask someone. Ask anyone," her brain was telegraphing. *Ask.*

She put out her hand to stop a woman wearing a fur cape with a lot of tails hanging down all around. "Gate A 11 . . . for New York . . . can you tell me which way it is?"

The woman withdrew her arm and brushed away an invisible something. "I'm sorry, but I haven't the faintest idea," she said, and moved on.

Bonnie Jo's eyes were so filled with tears she did not see the boy until he was standing directly in front of her.

"I couldn't help overhearing. I'm going that way. Here, let me take your suitcase. You know, we haven't got a lot of time."

She almost had to run to keep up with him, he was so tall and his legs so long.

Once, he said "You O.K.?" and that was all.

She nodded and on they went. She had no idea how far they'd come before he stopped and turning grinned at her. "Well, here we are. And in plenty of time after all. They've not even started to board yet."

He put down the suitcases. "Better get your ticket out. They're starting to move in there."

Inside the boarding area, everyone was standing. First-class passengers walking briskly toward the door designated for them; coach passengers moving in a polite but solid wedge toward theirs.

"Hold on tight," the boy said, "so I'll know you're there."

She couldn't help letting out a little squeak of laughter. In the rush, she had all but disappeared. The top of her head was inches below the tall boy's shoulder.

It was better once they were inside the sort of collapsible corridor that led into the plane. And it was better still, once they were inside the plane itself.

"Any seat in the second section," the stewardess said. A tall, slender girl with big brown eyes, she managed to look pretty even in the funny-looking cap she was wearing.

Not until then did it occur to Bonnie Jo that she and the boy might sit together. She almost hoped they wouldn't. It would be easier if she didn't have to talk to make up a lot of lies. Still . . . he was so nice-looking, though in a different kind of way. Maybe not quite a man yet, but not a boy either.

He moved confidently down the aisle ahead of her, then suddenly stopped and said "Thank you," sounding pleased.

Peering around, Bonnie Jo could see that the man with the goatee and beret who'd stood beside her in the airport had popped out of his seat and was bowing in the aisle.

The tall boy stowed their suitcases under their seats and watched as she tightened her seat belt. He grinned. "I bet I could put my two hands around your waist."

Bonnie Jo looked at his hands—big, long-fingered, with nice nails—and smiled back. "No bet." Flying might be fun with him beside her.

"First flight?"

She nodded.

He reached for her hand as if it were the most natural thing in the world to do and held it while the plane took off, then released it, not talking until the stewardess had made her little speech about oxygen masks and the pilot's voice had come crackling over the loudspeaker to tell them how high they would be flying and how fast. The weather in New York was cool and sunny.

Now, instead of a vaporous mass outside the window, the sun was shining. The sky was cloudless. Below, the countryside was marked out in shining squares of green and gold, transversed by tiny highways that stretched out like strands of ribbon. By looking far far ahead Bonnie Jo could see something that looked like a bit of mirror. She thought it might be Lake Michigan. The shadow of their plane was flying along below them.

Bonnie Jo closed her eyes. If she could just have flown on and on like this forever. With nothing ever changing. Even the baby within her would not be growing. Suspended between heaven and earth, everything was clear and clean and happy.

She must have slept because when she opened her eyes, the tall boy was smiling. "Now that you've had a little nap, it's time to introduce ourselves. I'm Joel Partridge. I'm on my way home from a wedding in Chicago. My cousin Henry's. He's one of the rich Partridges—bought me a round trip plane ticket just so I could be his best man—and I'm the *poorest* of the poor Partridges."

"Bonnie Jo . . . Jackson." She whispered her name without looking up.

"You'll have to do better than that." Joel Partridge's dark brown eyes, so deeply set that his forehead formed a little shelf above them, were amused. "Now that I've gone through the wear and tear of getting you on this plane, I'm not going to settle for just 'Bonnie Jo Jackson.' "

She looked down at her fingers twining in her lap. She did not know how to go on from there. Numbly, she shook her head.

"Should I guess?"

"If you want."

"I don't think I want." Suddenly he was serious.

"Somehow, I have the feeling that this isn't a time for games. You really are unhappy. Something is wrong, isn't it?"

"In . . . in a way." She could not look at him.

"Listen," Joel said. "I don't mean to be butting into something that isn't any of my business. No, that's not true. I *do* mean to. What I'm trying to say is—don't tell me if you don't want to—but back there in the airport, I was watching you. For ten, maybe fifteen minutes— you almost made me miss the plane—trying to decide to ask you . . . if I could help."

He stopped abruptly as the stewardess, coming down the aisle with a tray of soft drinks, stopped beside them.

Bonnie Jo shook her head. "Nothing, please."

"Nothing for me, either." Joel waited for the stewardess to move down the aisle. "But whatever it is, I want to help you. I mean, if I can. The funny thing, I usually don't go around . . . well, doing things like this. But if anybody's pushing you around . . ."

Tears blurred her vision. She could scarcely see as she fumbled with her seat belt. "I'll be back."

She made her way down the aisle. Iris, who had helped her think of almost everything, had not thought about her meeting people who would want to talk; that she would have to have a story to tell. Certainly, Iris hadn't thought about her meeting a boy she couldn't help liking.

Both the toilets were occupied when she got there. She waited for what seemed an interminable interval until a young woman carrying a baby in a hammock around her neck came out.

As soon as she was by herself, with the door closed and locked, she began to feel better. She stared at her image in the mirror above the tiny lavatory. She *was* pale. But to be pale was natural for her. "The color of skim milk, not even two percent," Mark had once laughingly described her skin. The faint blue smudges beneath her eyes only made them look bluer. But she was healthy. Healthier than her friend, Iris, who was always out of school with a cold or virus or something.

Bonnie Jo leaned forward, staring at herself until her breath fogged her image. Her mouth twisted into a smile. It was funny, really funny, that after Mark Truro and Bill Lobos, she should meet a boy she could really like without trying.

Someone was knocking sharply on the toilet door. Bonnie Jo said "Just a minute," but in possession of herself again, she did not hurry. She used the toilet, washed her hands, and brushed her hair. The knocking at the door had grown louder. Bonnie Jo opened it to face a woman with a firm jaw and an upswept hairdo.

"You're owning the toilet facilities?" the woman said icily, then shut herself inside.

On her way back to her seat, Bonnie Jo passed the man with the goatee and beret. He smiled and made a V with his fingers.

"I thought you were never coming back," Joel said. "I might have worried, except I've got a sister about your age who can tie up a bathroom for hours on end. She's eighteen. And you?"

"Almost. In June."

"Graduating?"

Bonnie Jo nodded, unable to keep from smiling because he was so persistent.

"Then what? College? A job? . . . Marriage?"

"Not the last. A job, most likely. I'm pretty good at shorthand and typing. There's a community college in Cedar City. I'd like to take a course or two there, at night."

Joel was nodding approvingly. "I knew you'd feel that way about college. How important it is. It's going to take me forever to get through CCNY—that's the College of the City of New York, if you don't happen to know. But unless you have parents who can afford to send you to college and on to graduate school or law school or whatever, you've got to do it by degrees. But you're going in the right direction, you can't help but get there." He flushed. "There I go again. You're the first girl I've ever talked to about myself. I can't explain it . . . except I somehow feel you understand."

Bonnie Jo blinked back a tear before it had time to show. It was the nicest thing any boy had ever said to her. Impulsively, she reached out her hand and clasped Joel's. Her fingers barely reached across his palm.

"We're coming in," he said.

The "Fasten Seat Belt" and "No Smoking" signs had been lighted. The stewardesses were returning passengers' wraps. The big plane seemed to be skimming the very tops of some low flat buildings, missing power lines only by inches.

Joel had taken a small notebook and a pencil from his pocket. "I'm working this afternoon, so I'll have to be on my way as soon as we land. Someone's meeting you?"

She stuttered for a moment, then almost without thinking the right words came. Straight from one of the true-life stories in *Romantic Love.* "My uncle. After my mother died, he and my aunt took care of me—they lived in Nebraska then—until my father married again. Now my aunt is sick, awfully sick. My uncle sent the money for me to come."

Joel nodded sympathetically. "That's rough. Seeing you, though, will do her more good than anything.

"Better give me their name and address," Joel said, his pencil poised. "Don't worry about the telephone number. I'll find it."

"You give me your name and your number. That would be better. I expect we . . . we'll be at the hospital a lot." That part had not been in *Romantic Love,* but it seemed the logical thing to say.

Joel printed his name, address, and telephone number on a piece of paper and gave it to Bonnie Jo. Grinning, he said "Don't lose it. It's not all that easy to find somebody in New York City."

The plane stopped. Passengers began surging down the aisles. The stewardesses, crisp in their uniforms and their uniform smiles, were saying "good-bye. . . . Have a nice day. . . . Good-bye. . . . Thank you for flying with us. . . . Good-bye . . ."

Bonnie Jo, a few steps ahead of Joel, was off the plane before him. Waiting, she saw the old couple that had flown with her from Cedar City, then the pretty girl with the long dark hair. She had not known that they were going to New York, too. Then as a large form blotted out her vision, Bonnie Jo's heart for a moment stopped beating as the woman in the purple pants suit brushed by her, muttering.

Joel looked puzzled. "What was that all about?"

Bonnie Jo shook her head and managed a little laugh. "Search me," she said. "I never saw her before in my life."

3 / Questions and Answers

"Job or no job," Joel said. "I'm not leaving you until your uncle gets here."

"But he'll come! He . . . he probably had trouble parking the car, that's all. Why would he have sent me the money to come unless he planned to meet me?" It was hard to keep her voice soft and reasonable when what she wanted was to cry out hysterically for Joel to leave her and be on his way. Already she had wasted ten minutes of valuable time trying to rid herself of this large young man who had appointed himself as her protector. Though she'd known about Eastern Standard Time, it still came as a shock that her appointment at the clinic was now less than an hour and a half away. "I . . . I don't want you to be late for work. I'd never forgive myself if I made you be late."

Joel, from his height, was staring around the waiting room. "What does your uncle look like? I think maybe I see him."

Bonnie Jo felt a quivering in her legs. She would not be able to keep it up much longer. "He . . . I . . . I haven't seen him for a long time. But he's not tall . . . nor short, either. But nice-looking . . . and he . . . he's got a lot of wavy dark hair. . . ."

Joel shook his head. "Too bad. I thought for a moment I had him."

A moment later, when Joel's prospect, a nice-looking man—neither short nor tall, but almost completely bald—appeared, Bonnie Jo put her hands over her face and sagged against Joel with helpless laughter.

It did something for both of them.

"O.K.," Joel said. "I'll go. If I hurry, I can still get to work on time. I've been promised the job of orderly at a hospital in Brooklyn, but I don't want to lose the job I've got until the new one opens up."

"Then get going!" Bonnie Jo said. "I'll be all right. I can take care of myself. I wasn't born yesterday, you know!"

"I guess you're right," Joel said, slowly.

Bonnie Jo shivered. For the first time he seemed really to be seeing her.

Then suddenly everything was all right again. "You can call me tonight," he said. "If you can. If you can't, well . . . I'll understand that. But I'm not going to say good-bye. One way or another, I'm going to see you before you leave New York." He put his arm lightly around her and kissed her forehead. "O.K.?"

"O.K."

He turned once before he reached the top of the down escalator and waved. She waited for five minutes before taking even a few steps forward. Even then, it seemed better to wait another interminable five minutes. Having gone through so much to keep the reason for her trip to New York from him, it seemed foolish to run the risk of seeing him when she went downstairs to look for a taxi.

There was no sign of him, however, and almost immediately a cab slid out from a waiting line and drew up to the curb where she was standing. The driver, short, heavy-set, and red-faced, leaned back to open the rear door of the cab but he did not get out. "That all your luggage, miss?" He tipped his head toward her small suitcase.

Bonnie Jo nodded and got in, putting the suitcase on the seat beside her. It was stifling inside the cab and she ran down the window on one side and lay her head back against the leather seat. All of her lifeblood seemed to have drained away.

The driver's voice roused her. "Not being given the gift of prophecy, miss, I'm afraid you'll have to tell me where you want to go."

"Oh ... oh ... I'm sorry. It's on East Seventy-eighth Street." She remembered that much. "I'll give you the exact number in a minute."

While she looked in her billfold for the piece of paper on which she'd written the address, the cab had circled its way out of the airport grounds and onto the highway, and it was traveling at such a speed that the wind, with the window opened, swept her voice away.

She closed the window and repeated the words and that time he must have heard for he continued with speed unabated. An interstate highway bisected Cedar City and people drove fast on that. But not as fast as people were driving here. Cars and trucks thundered past each other only to slow to an almost complete stop. And always the cab's meter kept running. The nice woman at Family Planning in Cedar City who'd helped her make arrangements had told her to ask the driver how much the fare would be before getting in the cab—some drivers were unscrupulous and would take advantage of the young or ignorant—but in her nervousness, she had forgotten.

Bonnie Jo stared at the back of the driver's neck. Fat, and red like his face, it was quilted with deep crevices. His picture stared back at her from his cab-driver's license, in its little frame tacked to the back of the front seat. His name was Timothy Walsh. She had thought he sounded Irish, and he was probably Catholic, too. At least, a small white plastic Madonna was fastened to the dashboard of the cab. She wondered if he knew where he was taking her. She didn't care. At least, he was not making conversation.

Even if she had been interested in her surroundings, the cab was moving much too fast for her to see much of anything except the huge apartments, most with dinky little balconies, and the grass, shrubs, and flowering trees bordering the highway on either side. Somehow, she had not thought there would be grass or trees at all in New York City. Then the realization shook her. They were not yet in the city. For suddenly, it was rising above her. All towers and turrets, cubes and pinnacles. It was a fairy kingdom rising mystically through a bluish gray haze.

For a moment and a moment only, Bonnie Jo allowed herself to think about how her first glimpse of New York might have been. She and Iris had talked about going there and how they would share a little apartment. But when they went to New York, they must go with a *skill*. Iris insisted on that. In both their cases, that meant shorthand and typing. Although the best of Miss Pomerantz's graduating seniors who'd been with her since sophomore year—she and Iris were among them—were very good indeed, it wasn't good enough. Miss Pomerantz stressed experience, too, before tackling a job away from home in a big city. Up in one corner of the blackboard in the Commercial Subjects room, Miss Pomerantz had written in her large, square handwriting: "Skill+Experience=Well-Paying Job."

As short a time as six months ago, Bonnie Jo had never thought she would be going to New York like this.

At the very thought of what lay ahead, her heart began beating faster and a sour taste of sickness born of fright rose in her mouth.

They were really in the city now. Crawling through streets so clogged with traffic the cab could barely move, it reached Park Avenue and again turning right shot off once more at an alarming rate of speed. Street signs whisked past. Sixty-fifth, Sixty-sixth, Sixty-seventh. The meter read seven dollars and seventy-five cents. She, herself, had read stories in the newspaper about dishonest cab drivers in New York, who took advantage of girls seeking abortions and demanded an astronomical fee. Anything between nine and ten dollars, however, the Family Planning woman had said, could be considered an honest fare.

A traffic light turned red, a dozen taxis came to a stop, huddled side by side and bumper to bumper. The light again changed to green and they all again assumed their frenetic speed.

At the next intersection Bonnie Jo's driver turned. This street was quieter. There were trees—small ones to be sure—planted in square holes in the wide sidewalk. A young woman was pushing a baby, with grocery sacks piled all around him, in a stroller. A well-dressed man was walking some kind of dog she'd never seen before.

The driver drew into the curb in front of a plain-looking brick building. On the white canvas canopy over the front door was printed the street number and the words "Women's Medical Arts." The meter read 9.45.

Bonnie Jo took two five-dollar bills from her billfold and fifty cents in change from a coin purse and handed it through the half-opened glass partition to the driver. He took the money and spat at her feet as she left the cab.

From behind a desk in the small lobby, a girl rose to meet Bonnie Jo. She was wearing neat-looking blue jeans, a white rib-knit "skinny" sweater. Her medium-brown hair was pulled back and tied to one side.

"Good morning!" she said, brightly. "Or, I should say, Good afternoon?" She glanced at her wrist watch, which was encased in a wide leather strap. "You're . . . ?"

"Bonnie Jo Jackson."

The girl, businesslike, whisked back again behind the desk and consulted a typed list that lay upon it. "Jackson, Jackson . . ." she said with a smile. "Yes. Yes, here we are. Bonnie Jo." She made a check with a ball-point pen. "You're a little early, but that's fine. Better to be early than late. When one's flying in from a distance, it's difficult to keep things right on the dot." She paused, then shook her head almost reprovingly. "You're crying. And you mustn't. Everything is going to be all right."

Sympathy was more than she could stand. "It's not that," she mumbled. "I'm not afraid . . . really. It's just that . . . that everybody knows. A woman on the plane knew . . . by looking at me. The cab driver . . . I . . . I can't tell you what he did."

"Stupid people," the girl said. "Pay no attention to them. Now, if you'd like to come with me."

The elevator into which the receptionist led her was small and of the self-service type. A button was punched for the sixth and top floor and the cubicle moved slowly upward.

"This is the laboratory," the girl said when the door opened. "All that happens here are just the routine blood tests. To find out, among other things, if you're Rh negative. About fifteen percent of all women are, you know. We're very careful about that. In case sometime an Rh neg. would *want* to have a baby."

Wanting to have a baby was something Bonnie Jo had never thought about. Some people must, or else there wouldn't be all those people waiting in line, so to speak, to adopt someone else's baby. The counselor she'd talked to in Cedar City had told her about the waiting list. Not to influence her, she'd said, but just in case she had wanted to have it. Like Gloria Pardekooper.

Just thinking about Gloria Pardekooper took some of the fear away. But not all. As the elevator bearing the receptionist dropped from sight, another girl, similarly dressed, rose to meet her. Somewhere along the line Bonnie Jo had expected a nurse. At least, somebody dressed in white. But that was foolish. An abortion now was an everyday sort of thing. Not a nurse-doctorish situation at all. Even so, someone like Mrs. Martin, the school nurse, with her stiff-starched bosom and heavy-soled white shoes would have made her feel better.

"Prick," the new girl said as she plunged a needle into a blue vein in the crook of Bonnie Jo's arm.

"I . . . I didn't bleed," Bonnie Jo whispered. It seemed an ill omen.

"Only because I didn't hit the vein," the laboratory girl mumbled. "You must have thick skin. Well, I guess we'd better give it another try. *Prick.*"

This time Bonnie Jo felt a sharp stab of pain and dark red blood began to fill the slender glass tube.

The girl smiled. "Well, that's all that happens here.

Take the elevator down one floor. Miss Glynn is in charge down there. She'll explain what happens next."

As Bonnie Jo turned to leave, she saw that three more people had arrived to have a blood sample taken. Two were girls—one looked younger than she did, Bonnie Jo thought—and the other was a woman as old as, or older than, her mother.

She heard the word "Prick!" brightly spoken as she walked toward the elevator.

The girl at the desk, dressed as casually as those Bonnie Jo had met before, handed her two sheets of paper stapled together at the top. "Just some questions for you to answer. But it's not like an examination you take at school. Your answers don't have to be long and we don't grade you on it." She smiled confidentially. "It just helps us spot any emotional problems you might have, so we can talk them over. Beforehand."

She waved a hand toward one of the molded plastic chairs that sat around the room. All were gaily colored and a writing surface was attached to each. In more than half of the dozen chairs, women and girls were busily writing.

Holding her breath, Bonnie Jo crossed to the far end of the room where she saw an empty chair. Not until she saw what the questions were would she be able to breathe without a small, sharp pain knifing up under her breastbone.

Her eyes skimmed the first page of questions. They all seemed to be concerned with her medical history. Childhood illnesses? Allergic reactions? Age and health of parents? Vaccinations, innoculations. These were all things she could answer. The pain under her breast-bone had started to subside. In her small, neat hand-writing, she finished the first page and turned to the second.

"Why do you think termination of pregnancy is best for you now?"

"Because," she wrote, then paused, the pencil growing moist in her hand. The girl at the desk had said she could keep the answers short. She had not said that they need be truthful.

She pushed back wisps of hair from her damp forehead and stared at the blank space on the page, then began to write.

"I think it is best for me now because I couldn't have given it away. I would have kept it and given it all I could. But I realized that wouldn't be much. It wouldn't have been fair to the baby."

She read over what she had written. Part of it was true. The part about not giving it away and about keep-ing it and giving it the best she could. But that was before she'd thought about abortion. Rather, it was before Merle, her stepfather, had thought about it for her. In spite of all the scenes, in spite of the fact that he was thinking only about himself and what people would think about *him* and what it would do to his contracting business, it was the only way out she could think of for herself. The only way.

Next had come getting the money, making the appointment. After that, all she thought she had to do was go to New York and have it ... not be made to answer a lot of prying questions. "How have you been related to the man in this pregnancy? Does he know? What doubts or fears do you have? How has this pregnancy affected your relationship with him? When you first learned you were pregnant, what were your feelings and your thoughts?"

Prying! What difference did it make? It was all over and done with, or would be as soon as the doctor did it to her. Then she could start forgetting the past. She could forget that Mark, whom she once had loved —and had lost through no fault of her own—now belonged to Sis Claiborne. When the hateful growing thing Bill Lobos had put inside her had been destroyed, then she could start forgetting Bill Lobos. To keep the tears from coming, she pressed the heels of both hands against her eyes until colored lights danced behind them.

Someone jogged her elbow. "Hey, none of that." The voice was friendly, almost as coarse as a boy's.

Bonnie Jo looked at the girl who'd addressed her from the next chair. She was wearing a synthetic blond wig—no hair could have looked like that—too much makeup and false eyelashes carelessly applied. However, the eyes that looked out from behind them were not only clear and beautiful, but of astonishing blueness.

"Don't let it bug you, baby. I've been through it before—right here at this clinic. So I know all about it. The waiting, answering the stupid questions. Still, it's a good deal, even if they are making a fortune. You figure it out. Fifty abortions a day, seven days a week, at a hundred dollars a whack. I'm just hoping I get the same doctor—young, good-looking, a real swinger. Maybe you'll get him too. When he's through with you and you're crawling down off the table, he gives you a big grin and a swat on the behind and says, 'O.K., you're not pregnant anymore,' and that's all there is to it."

She scraped her chair a bit closer to Bonnie Jo's. "The thing I hate is that I'm so stupid. But that's Claressa Fogle for you. Has to do everything the hard way. But enough's enough. They've seen the last of me around *this* place. And if you're smart, they'll have seen the last of you—though if either of us had any brains we would never have had to come here in the first place."

The girl who'd given Bonnie Jo the questionnaire, absent from the room while Claressa was talking, had returned and was coming toward them. She put her hand reassuringly on Bonnie Jo's shoulder and smiled. "If you're having trouble with your questions, perhaps you'd better let *me* do the counseling."

When Bonnie Jo shook her head, Miss Glynn turned to Claressa. "If you've finished, the doctor will see you now."

From behind the false eyelashes, thick as rushes around a lake, Claressa Fogle winked a clear, bright blue eye.

4 / Wolves Live in the Woods

If she wrote it all down just the way it happened, Bonnie Jo thought, it would make a book.

And it would start, of course, with Mark Truro. Just as, in a way, it had started with him, it had ended because of him.

Certainly, if he hadn't picked her up that afternoon after school when she was standing in the pouring down rain on the corner of Fourteenth and Chester, waiting for the bus, they'd never have become acquainted at all.

But he *had* stopped. The car pulled up to the curb, and he had leaned over to shout out the window, "Get in. I'll take you wherever you're going. Five minutes more in this downpour, and nobody would be able to *find* you!"

She got in the car. "I live out by the Plaza."

Shivering, she began picking at the thin stuff her dress was made of, so it wouldn't cling so to her body. She might as well have had nothing on at all.

"I'm Mark Truro."

As if she didn't know! You didn't have to know Mark Truro to know who he was. He was one of the handful of seniors who, ever since sophomore year, had got elected to class office or the Student Senate. He'd been one of the three representatives from Central

High to meet with kids from the other four high schools to try to figure out ways to avoid the violence that was always breaking out after some of the night football or basketball games around the city. After his name in *The Centaur,* the junior yearbook, there was a long paragraph listing all the organizations he belonged to. Even Hi Y and Glee Club. Things like that.

"Bonnie Jo Jackson," when she spoke, it came out in such a series of little shivering bubbles that they both had laughed.

"Sounds as if you might be a li'l ol' So'thrun gal." He grinned. "You a li'l ol' So'thrun gal?"

She shook her head. "No, but my father came from Mississippi. His family moved up North when he was still a little boy."

She was warmer now. The first stop light they'd come to, he'd reached around into the back seat for a wadded-up Turkish towel.

"Tennis towel," he'd said. "It's pretty dirty, but it will help dry you off a little."

She'd dried her face and arms and legs, then rubbed the dripping ends of her long fair hair.

"It's a nice name, in any case," he said. "I've seen you around, you know."

"Mark's a nice name, too."

"At our house, you can just about take your choice of names. I've a brother, Matthew. He's the oldest, as you might guess. Then after me, comes Luke and John. But that isn't all. There's a snapper. I've a sister. My mother wanted to name her Paula, but my father said enough was enough. Her name is Jane."

Bonnie Jo forced a little laugh. "I've a little sister, too. Lucinda. Her nickname is 'Precious.' " No need to tell Mark Truro, who obviously was proud of his family, that Lucinda was not really her sister at all. She was Merle's daughter and had come to live with them at the time he'd married her mother. Calling her "Precious" was the biggest joke of the year. She should have been called "Obnoxious."

Traffic moved more slowly as they neared the huge shopping center known as the Plaza. Her house was now only a few blocks away. Soon it would all be over.

"Turn right at the next corner," Bonnie Jo directed, "then I'll tell you when to stop."

It was a street of houses built maybe twenty-five years before. Undistinguished but comfortable, you could almost tell what kinds of people lived in them, Bonnie Jo thought, by the way their yards were kept. Most had lawns that were already smooth and green and glistened in the spring rain, the early tulips standing stiff as soldiers in their borders. In others yards the grass grew patchily or not at all. Upended tricycles, coaster wagons, or toys were strewn about.

"Ours is the fourth house from the corner," Bonnie Jo said. "I'm afraid you can't get in the driveway because of the gravel and the sand. We're fixing it up. Building a room on in the back. My stepfather's a contractor and doing the work himself."

There, it was out—about having a stepfather. But

it was better that way. She didn't want Mark Truro to think that her own father, who had come from Mississippi and, himself, had named her Bonnie Jo, would have a driveway full of sand and gravel and cement blocks that anybody, at a glance, could tell had not just been hauled in yesterday.

"My mother says, 'The shoemaker's children never have any shoes, and contractor's wives never get anything done to their own houses.'"

"I know how that is. My father's a doctor, and whenever any of us kids gets sick or anything, he makes us go to another doctor." Rain was still bucketing against the windshield as Mark drew the car into the curb.

Bonnie Jo looked out at the rain, but did not move.

"I guess I'd better hop out."

"You'll get wet. . . ."

It was such a ridiculous thing to say they both laughed.

"You could wait, you know," Mark said, "until it lets up a little."

Bonnie Jo shook her head. "Thank you. I'll be fine, really. I'll just make a quick dash."

"Well, at least you don't have to worry about your school books getting wet. Look at what I brought home with me."

Bonnie Jo glanced at the leather zippered case and pile of books that lay on the seat between them. "I was lucky," she said. "I had a double study period today and finished all I had to do." Not that she couldn't have done more. A little extra work on the character sketch Miss Hartsung had assigned for English most likely would have resulted in a B, or even a B+, instead of the C she would undoubtedly get. She had skimmed the chapter on the Civil War for American History, filed a few dates, and digested what seemed to be most important. If learning hadn't come so easily, maybe she would have tried harder. But except for shorthand and typing—and being good at those subjects would help her get a job and furnish an escape—what was the use?

Somehow, right now, it didn't seem so smart not to have brought any books home at all.

She put her hand on the latch of the car door. "Well," she said. "Here I go."

"Wait. Take the towel. It will furnish a little protection."

"No," she said, then on impulse took it, putting it over her head and holding it fast beneath her chin.

"You look like a sister. A nun, I mean. The way they used to look."

"That's a nice compliment," she could tell she was blushing. It was one of the foolish things she did and could not help doing.

Before he could reply she was out of the car, skirting little piles of sand and gravel that Precious had carried to new locations.

"It's for you," her mother said as she came into the kitchen. "It's a boy."

Bonnie Jo wiped her hands. Someone who had

lived in the house before them had installed a dishwasher but it didn't work, and now, even when you opened the door, it emitted a sour stale smell.

Although the phone was in the back hallway, there was still no way to prevent her stepfather from listening. He sat in his Reclina-Chair, in the far back position, looking at her over the top of the newspaper. Merle moved his lips when he read. She had always thought that was a joke until after the divorce and her mother married Merle. But moving his lips didn't mean that he was stupid.

"Is this the home of a li'l ol' So'thrun gal, name of Bonnie Jo? Her pa, Ah believe, came from Mississippi?"

Her heart performed an unexpected somersault. "Mark?" she said. *"Mark?"* Hearing his voice, she still could not believe it. Iris, to whom she had confided everything that afternoon in Iris's little bedroom up under the eaves in their big old house, would not believe it either when she told her.

"I thought twenty-four hours would be long enough for you to develop double pneumonia, the plague, or whatever, so I thought I ought to call and check up."

"I haven't even *sneezed.*" She laughed. It was a shared joke. "I guess that comes from giving Red Cross swimming lessons in the rain all last summer. Those little children, with their blue lips, at least half of them frightened to death of the water, splashing around . . ." Maybe, someday, if she were lucky, she would be able to tell Mark about the little boy, not more than six or seven, who—one day when she'd forgotten to bring a towel—had divided *his,* spreading a piece of it over one of her legs because he thought that she was cold. . . .

"It wasn't easy finding you, you know," Mark Truro said. Suddenly, he seemed embarrassed, but his natural "naturalness" righted it again. "I knew what your name was. But I didn't know the name of your stepfather. So, I had to do a bit of sleuthing to find out how to get in touch with you."

"But you did," she said, wondering but not wanting to ask how he had found out.

"Never underestimate the powers of a Truro, particularly when he has a *purpose.* If you haven't a date next Saturday night, maybe we could roam around. You know. See what's up?"

"I'd love to!" Her heart was pounding. For over a year now, she hadn't gone out with a boy she really liked. Not that there'd been anything really wrong with either Tom Grabar or Tony Farmer. But they were just boys. Not that she was brighter than they were—though she was—or not that she had more ambition. She didn't. Tom Grabar planned to go to work for the telephone company as a linesman apprentice when he graduated. And Tony Farmer was going to trade school and learn to be a welder.

"Well, if it's O.K., then, I'll pick you up around eight?"

"Yes!"

"But maybe before then, I'll see you at school.

Right now, my sister Jane is breathing down my neck saying I'm using her phone, that it's in her name in the phone book, and that I have to hang up."

Bonnie Jo heard a girlish squeal at the other end of the line and the connection was broken. She hung up the receiver, still hardly believing it was Mark who'd called.

Before she was half way back to the kitchen, Merle bellowed, "Who was that and what did he want?" from the living room. When she didn't answer, he appeared in the doorway. "You'll answer when you're spoken to," he said.

"I didn't hear you," she said, trying to keep from wincing as he approached her. For the first year after Merle Binder and her mother were married, he hadn't touched her, but during the last few months he had once struck her on the cheek, where she had carried the imprint of his hand over an entire weekend. On another occasion, he had seized her wrist and held her arm behind her back until she had sunk crying to the floor.

"Mark Truro."

"Truro?" Now it seemed to be Merle who was hard of hearing. "Son of *the* Truro, the fat-cat doctor? You going out with him?"

Bonnie Jo shrugged, although she knew the gesture was enraging to Merle. "Mark's not a doctor yet. But I guess maybe his father, Marcus Truro, is."

"Marcus Truro," Merle said. The red in his face had begun to subside. "Well. He's on the Zoning Commission, too, you know."

"I guess. I don't know." This was not the truth. If you read the papers at all, you knew that Marcus Truro was usually the single hold-out. Sometimes, he won his point just because of his sheer stubbornness—his failure to give in if he thought his cause was right.

Merle said "Humph," then looked her up and down. Turning around to walk away he added, "When's all this supposed to happen?"

"Saturday."

In the interest of peace she had supplied the answer.

Since then, in the almost nine months she had been dating Mark Truro, everything had gone so smoothly she had scarcely dared believe it. The night Mark had come to pick her up, the living room had been miraculously cleared beforehand of the always over-filled ashtrays and piles of his ratty-looking magazines that Merle allowed no one to touch, as if anybody wanted to. Even more important, Precious—either through bribery or the almost hypnotic influence that Merle was able to exercise over his daughter—was in bed or, at least, out of sight.

After that night, she and Mark had gone everywhere together. Or almost everywhere. She knew there were parties Mark went to and to which she wasn't invited. (Some of the big ones, for instance, you couldn't *miss* hearing about.) Rosemary Ramekin, who was one of *the* girls in the senior class just as Mark was one of *the* boys, had had one, and so had Dorian Hawley. Mark, who had gone to both—probably to some others, as well, that she didn't know about—had explained how it was.

"It's this kind of new thing," he'd said apologetically, "to have parties where kids don't go in couples. If it's a girl who's having the party she just invites the girls and guys she'd like to come and then they mix it up after they get there. If it's a guy having the party, it works the same way."

They'd been to a movie and were sitting in Mark's car in front of Bonnie Jo's house. When he told her about the party Sis Claiborne was having and that he was going, it was a long time before she said anything. Then she said, "I see," though she didn't see it at all. It seemed to her that if two people were going together, they'd want to *be* together no matter who was having a party.

She moved ever so slightly away from him so she could not feel the weight of his arm on her shoulder. That did nothing at all, however, to lighten the leaden weight that had lodged itself at the base of her throat.

"You see how it is, don't you, Bon-Bon?" He took his free hand and turned her face toward his, but she pulled away. "No," she said. "I don't. If I'm not invited, I don't see why you have to go at all."

Her tone was so childishly surly that he laughed. "Don't make something out of nothing. I've known Sis Claiborne since we went to Country Day School kindergarten. I think I've been to every birthday party she ever had. Our families have had cottages next door to each other at the lake ever since I can remember."

"Still," she said. "I don't see why, if she has a party, you *have* to go. . . ."

"I don't have to. I want to. She . . . they're my friends."

"And who am I?"

"You're my girl. You're my Bon-Bon."

This time when he drew her close she let him kiss her. And as it always happened, she could feel her love for him welling up, overflowing until it almost seemed that she should die of happiness.

Silently, he let her out of the car and walked with her up to the door, then taking the key from her hand opened it. She stepped inside but he did not follow her as he usually did for one more long, deep, sweet kiss that seemed to melt their bodies into one. Instead, he pressed her hand until she could feel an electric current dancing in her palm then turned and went down the walk to his car.

Listening, she watched until he merged with the shadows. He was whistling. Very softly. Under his breath.

Bonnie Jo hardly ever saw Mark at school. He was in advanced track in all his classes—math, English, chemistry, and history. Commercial subjects, of which she was taking three, were all in another part of the building.

After school, Mark nearly always had a meeting of some kind, tennis practice, or a swimming meet. Something. So usually she went home with Iris Beason who lived on the same bus line.

That's what they were doing one afternoon when Iris told Bonnie Jo there'd been a big story in the *Sunday Gazette,* a paper Merle didn't take, about Sis Claiborne's birthday party. It was to be at the Plantation, a big public dance pavilion just outside the city limits. Name bands and rock groups performed there when they came to town, and Sis's parents had rented it especially for the occasion.

There was a full page of pictures, too, Iris went on, showing Sis and Dorian Hawley and Rosemary Ramekin climbing around on ladders, hanging Japanese lanterns, and covering the ceiling with big festoons of crepe paper. Tables with big beach umbrellas over them were already in place. The story accompanying the pictures said entertainment was to be continuous. There'd be music for dancing as well as music for listening. And, she added, for making out . . . though the story didn't say so in those exact words.

"The woman who wrote it all up was pretty excited," Iris said wryly. "Seems we don't have 'coming out' parties in Cedar City *every* day. If you ask *me,* Sis Claiborne has been 'out' for somebody since she was in the sixth grade. And now that Craig What's-his-name moved away, she's out for Mark Truro. If I were you, Bonnie Jo, I'd watch it."

She stood up, a cheerful girl with a mop of too-curly auburn hair and gray-green eyes, pressed the button for her street corner which was approaching, and a minute later was gone.

The bus lurched on. Almost a mile beyond her own stop, Bonnie Jo gazed blindly through the bus window at unfamiliar surroundings. A block further on, she got off.

It was not awfully cold for January, but that morning she had not dressed herself for a mile-long walk. Within minutes, she was so cold that the concentration demanded simply to put one foot ahead of the other blocked from her mind the significance of what Iris had told her.

Not until later that night, with the dishes done and Precious bathed and read to and put to bed, could she really think. It was over. She knew it. Everything between her and Mark Truro was *over*—the word was italicized in her mind—unless, as Iris who was her friend had suggested, she would "watch it!"

The sign, "Watch it!" appeared throughout the night in her dreams. Pickets marching bore signs that said "Watch it!" Headlines appeared in newspapers, flashed across gigantic television screens. "Watch it!" In color.

Watching it, however, did no good at all. A week passed. She did not see Mark at school, which was not surprising, but neither did he call. Then, though she knew she was making a mistake, she called him. When he came to the phone and she heard his voice, she was

61

so nervous that Mark had to say "hello" twice before she could speak.

"I thought maybe you were sick," she said at last. "I hadn't heard from you." She tried not to sound accusing.

"Not sick. Just busy. I'm taking the College Board examination in a couple of weeks so I'm hitting the books pretty hard."

She was the one who had to break the silence that followed. "Did you have a good time at the birthday party?"

"Birthday party?" He paused, as if it took him time to comprehend. "Oh, Sis Claiborne's party. Yeah, yeah. It was great."

Without warning, she was crying.

"Bon-Bon, Bon-Bon baby. It isn't anything to cry about. I told you how it was. I explained . . ."

She drew in her breath in a little sob and held it until she could safely speak. "I'm not going to see you again, am I?"

"See me! Of course, you're going to see me. You could see me now. I'd come right this minute, if I could. But I'll see you soon. That's a promise."

In her relief, laughing and crying all at once, she whispered "good-bye" and hung up the receiver—so she would not seem quite as foolish as she was.

A hundred times, a thousand times, Bonnie thought that if she hadn't gone to a basketball game it would never have happened. But when Iris called and asked if she wouldn't like to go with her and Gordy Pinter, she'd said yes.

Even then, it probably would never have happened, if she had been sitting anyplace in the huge gym except directly in front of Mark and Sis Claiborne— and not sitting next to the dark-complexioned, thin-faced boy with the hooded eyes.

She would have moved away, but there was no place to go.

Before the game started, Mark, looking embarrassed, said "hello" while Sis pretended to engage in spirited conversation with someone in the bench behind.

Throughout the first quarter, Bonnie Jo stared out at the basketball court seeing nothing, hearing nothing —except Sis laughing too shrilly and commenting too loudly on this play or that.

The whistle blew, cutting through Bonnie Jo's brain like a surgical instrument.

Beside her, Iris whispered fiercely, "Laugh! Talk to me! Talk to that boy next to you! But do something, do anything to show Mark Truro you don't care—or to give *her* any satisfaction."

The dark-complexioned boy with the hooded eyes was leaning toward her from the other side. His lips were thin but as elaborately sculpted as those on the marble head of Caesar that sat on a pedestal at the back of the school library. "Your little friend has the right idea, baby. Only don't talk to *her*. Talk to me."

When he reached for her hand, she let him take it.

Even when everybody got to his feet and screamed and yelled during moments of excitement, he did not let go.

At the half, he said "Tell your little friend we're leaving," then as if he were afraid Bonnie Jo would not do as he asked, he spoke to Iris himself. "This game's a drag. I think the two of us will go someplace where we can have a little fun. Don't worry, I'll see she gets home all right."

Already he had pulled Bonnie Jo to her feet and boosted her up the steep step behind them. Then, though it would have been easier to go the other way, with elaborate apologies and requests to be excused, he tramped in front of Mark Truro and Sis Claiborne, finally reaching the aisle.

For a moment Bonnie Jo was afraid that Iris would follow. Then she decided that fear was foolish. Iris was the one who, in the first place, had advised her to "watch it." Iris was the one who had told her to laugh, to talk, to do anything to prove to Mark that she didn't care.

In the cold still air outside the building Bonnie Jo began to laugh. "Here I am, letting you take me home and I don't even know your name!"

Dark eyes glinted beneath the hooded lids and he smiled his sculptured smile. "It's no secret," he said. "Lobos. Bill Lobos."

The car into which he rather gallantly handed her was low-slung, racy, its rear end angled upward. It was the kind of a car a boy who is a good mechanic can put together so it is his very own. "Do you know what 'Lobos' means—in Spanish?"

Bonnie Jo shook her head. Her body was quivering in a queer sort of way, a mingling of fear and excitement.

"Wolf," the dark boy said. "That's what my name was before I changed it. That's what 'Lobos' means—*wolf.*"

His arm around her shoulder, he started the car and turned it out into the street.

"I live out by the Plaza." Her voice was the barest whisper.

"Interesting," the dark boy said, "but *I* don't. Wolves live in the woods."

5 / A Miscalculated Risk

Bonnie Jo did not know how much time had elapsed since Claressa, winking a bright blue eye, had departed. Still, it had been time enough for the two girls and the older woman she had seen in the laboratory upstairs to arrive and begin to fill out their questionnaires.

She had written nothing.

Aware that the girl at the desk was watching her, though pretending not to, Bonnie Jo passed a hand across her moist forehead and again stared down at the unanswered questions.

"How have you been related to the man in this pregnancy?"

Time was passing. The girl at the desk showed signs of getting up and coming over. With the pen sticky in her hand, Bonnie Jo began to write.

"If you mean by 'related,' am I married to him, I am not. He is just someone I know." She read over what she had written, then crossed out the word "know," substituting for it the word "knew."

But that was only the beginning. New, probing questions, each opening an old but still unhealed wound, leapt up at her from the page.

"Does the man related to this pregnancy know of your condition? If he knows, is he aware of the course of action you plan to take?"

"How has this pregnancy affected your relationship with him? What doubts or fears do you have?"

"When you first learned you were pregnant, what were your feelings and your thoughts?"

Bonnie Jo's mind spun backward to the day she had told Iris everything that had happened. Well perhaps, she hadn't told Iris *everything*. For example, about the getting drunk part; that was buried so deeply in her subconscious that she never wanted to think about it again. Besides, the getting drunk part Iris would have understood least of all.

Iris, her "sunspots"—she refused to call them freckles—standing out on a face suddenly as white as if it had been bleached in Clorox, had, for a moment, looked as if she might faint.

"But you didn't!" Iris cried. "You couldn't! Not . . . not with Bill Lobos!"

Of course, the girls' toilet, on a Monday morning between classes with the bell just about to ring, had not been the place to tell her. But she had. And Iris, once the whole impact of the thing had really penetrated, had been full of advice. "The first thing to do is tell him," Iris had said. "After all, it's his fault—or, at least, it's his fault as much as it is yours and he ought to know. Maybe you could get married and then divorced. Not being a Catholic doesn't make it as tough on you as it would on me."

Although Iris was her best friend, sometimes she almost hated her. And she had almost hated her then. What did Iris know about it? Iris had a mother and father who loved each other. Iris ate at a table where an extra place was always set, just in case she or one of the other kids wanted to bring someone home for dinner. What did Iris know about anything?

So she hadn't taken Iris's advice. About that, anyway. She hadn't told Bill Lobos anything. She couldn't have told him if she'd wanted to. That day in the car, he'd said that the police had been watching his house and that he was going to be moving on.

Painful as thinking back had been, it had at least provided an answer for the question. Quickly now, she began to write. "The man related to this pregnancy does not know of my condition because I did not tell him." It was easier to use their words than try to phrase it in her own way. "The way it has affected my relationship with him is to make me never want to see him again. If I had a baby, I would not want him to be its father."

Biting into her lip, she took a deep breath, expelled it and continued writing. "The only doubts or fears that I have is that I might die and that other people would learn that was the reason. Then everything would be for nothing. Before that, though, when I first learned I was pregnant, I thought that if a certain boy found out I would kill myself. I was afraid, too, that if my stepfather found out he would beat me, maybe even kill me. I do not think so much about dying now. All I want now is to get it over with and go back home and start living my life again."

That was all. She was through. She wiped her

damp hands with a little wad of tissue she found in her purse then took the completed questionnaire to the young woman as she had seen the others do.

A sign on the desk said her name was Miss Glynn. She was wearing a large yellow button with a Charlie Brown face. As Bonnie Jo looked at it, the face disappeared and the word "Smile" came in its place.

Miss Glynn's eyes, skimming first one page, and then the next, looked up. "There are no right or wrong answers to these questions, as I'm sure you know. We ask them to find out a little more about you. 'Crisis Intervention,' we call it. We don't want anyone to be sorry. Afterward, that is. Sometimes, in talking things over a girl changes her mind. In fact, a girl who was in here earlier in the day decided to go home and have her baby and to heck with the neighbors.

"Sometimes, interviews reveal that a girl is being pushed into an abortion by the man. Other times, we find out that the girl herself really wants to terminate her pregnancy, but has been afraid to admit it. Both situations can cause trouble later on."

She looked up. "Has anything like that happened to you?"

If she'd been a better liar, she might have tried. But with the counselor eyeing her rather narrowly, the truth seemed better. "My stepfather and my mother wanted me to have the abortion—though they didn't give me the money. My own father *didn't* want me to have it, but gave me the money anyway. It doesn't matter about them, though. *I'm* the one who wants to have it."

The counselor smiled. "That being the case, I'll tell you about the method we use here at the clinic. Vacuum aspiration, it's called. Sometimes, the suction method. Vacuum aspiration is safer, because there's less chance of infection or hemorrhage. It's also less painful than the more common 'dilation and curettage,' where the fetus is scraped from the walls of the womb . . ."

Bonnie Jo could feel moisture gathering on her forehead and a misty sweep of darkness passed before her eyes. "I don't care how they do it."

"We still think it's best for you to know," Miss Glynn said, sweetly. "In vacuum aspiration, there is no cutting or scraping. The cervix, the entrance to the uterus, is dilated or opened in the same way, but instead of a knife, the doctor uses a small stainless steel vacuum curette to empty the contents of the womb with two or three minutes of carefully controlled suction . . ."

Bonnie Jo averted her eyes, in case Miss Glynn should by trying to show her the horrid thing; she willed herself not to hear, but it did no good. In bits and snatches, the words came through. ". . . Rounded end . . . less bleeding . . . likelihood . . . puncturing . . . uterine wall. And that," she concluded cheerily, "is our little story. In five minutes, it's all over. Afterward, you may rest for a while if you're feeling a little woozy. The nurse, that's Mrs. Whey, will give you an antibiotic to avert any possible infection and some pills to control bleeding, and after that, you're on your way! Now, if you'll just come along with me, the doctor will see you shortly."

The cubicle into which she was ushered was no bigger than a telephone booth, its only furnishing a small straight-backed chair. On it lay a white something wrapped in clear plastic.

"Hospital gown," said the mini-skirted nurse—who must be Mrs. Whey—who had greeted her when she got off the elevator. "*And* scuffs. Take off all your clothes, put on the gown and scuffs and wait until I come for you. It will be a few minutes before the doctor is ready. For some reason, the one in there now is taking longer than usual."

Claressa Fogle, Bonnie Jo thought. *Claressa Fogle, with the bright blue eyes ... was Claressa Fogle taking longer?*

"Oh, by the way," the nurse was going on. "You needn't worry about your belongings, your purse and things. Everything will be perfectly safe. Nobody comes to this floor unless Miss Glynn brings them."

Bonnie Jo's fingers fumbled with the zipper of her dress and the hooks on her brassiere. Then with nothing on but her pantyhose, she tugged to open the packet that held the gown. It turned out to be made of a heavy, crepe-like paper and reached to her ankles. The scuffs were made for feet almost twice her size.

She perched on the side of the chair on which she'd

placed her neatly folded clothes. From someplace far off in the building, she could hear the faint ringing of the phone. Other than that, there was no sound at all except the dull pounding of her heart.

"For some reason, this one's taking longer," the nurse had said. But *this* long? thought Bonnie Jo. *Something had gone wrong.* She could feel her mouth drying out with fear. Yet, perhaps not as much time had elapsed as it seemed. She had no way of knowing. She counted the heavy, thudding beatings of her heart trying to gauge the passing minutes.

Four hundred beatings. Five minutes. She got up and, pulling aside the curtain, looked out. No one. Nothing. Except a stairway leading down, the elevator, and two sets of double doors, two other doors, all closed.

In panic, she darted back to her cubicle but before her fumbling, icy fingers could untie the tapes of the paper gown, the nurse was pushing aside the curtain to the small room. "All ready?" Her tone was cheery and professional. "It's not too late to change your mind, you know. . . ."

"Claressa Fogle?" Bonnie Jo's voice quavered on the name.

"Claressa?" She gave Bonnie Jo a quick penetrating look then laughed. "If that's what's bothering you, don't give it another thought. Claressa Fogle's fine. Just fine. The doctor has done another one since her."

Bonnie Jo pushed aside the curtain and said, "I'm ready then, I guess," and in her paper scuffs and nightgown followed the brisk, starched figure of Mrs. Whey down the hall toward the large double doors.

Short, slight, with the kind of pale eyebrows and eyelashes that tend toward invisibility, he didn't look like a doctor at all. At least, he didn't look like any of the doctors Bonnie Jo had had any experience with in real life. Nor, for that matter, on television, either.

Certainly, the outfit he was wearing—baggy pants, a kind of smock and cap shaped like a layer cake, all in the color of split pea soup—made it hard to think of him, as Claressa Fogle did, as a swinger. Maybe he wasn't hers.

Even the room in which it was going to happen wasn't at all like she had thought it would be. Smaller, almost cramped, there was little in it except the operating table, covered with a white paper sheet. And crazily, the stirrup things in which she was supposed to put her feet wore pot-holder mittens made of flowered chintz. In pink and green.

Later, it would seem strange that in the brief second after she entered the room she should have seen so much. Stranger still, that all fear seemed to have left her. It was as if her true self had stepped outside her body, leaving a shell that looked like her but had no thoughts or feelings of its own.

"Jackson?" the doctor said. He looked down at a clip board with a sheaf of papers attached. "Bonnie Jo? Seventeen?"

His voice was surprisingly deep. And he sounded nice. It seemed only right to smile.

"And I'm Dr. Ochre," he added. They might have been meeting at a party. Bonnie Jo would not have been surprised had he offered to shake hands.

"Well, then," he said. "You're next. Climb up on the table and maintain your dignity the best you can."

There was a step at one end, rather high, and he put his hand under her left elbow to help her up. "There's not much of you, is there?" He didn't say it in the same way Joel Partridge did—how strange that she should think of him then—but grinned, adding, ". . . though there is probably more of you than you wish there were."

She was on the table, surrounded by a white clear light whose source she could not determine.

"I think I'd better examine you, though, before I have Mrs. Whey 'prep' you."

She could feel the doctor's fingers on her abdomen, lightly touching, then pressing firmly here, then there, but so briefly that she could not be sure that he had touched her at all.

Soon it would happen. She would be given a pain pill and a paracervical block, whatever that was, though Miss Glynn had told her, she had forgotten. A sheet would be suspended over the table so that she could see the doctor's face, but never see a drop of blood or an instrument. Even if it hurt a little, it wouldn't hurt for long. Who had told her that? Or was it something she had read? In a magazine, perhaps. But after the hurt had passed, the shiny instruments—that she had never seen—put down, the sound of running water heard no more, the doctor would say, "Well, that's it. You're not pregnant anymore."

But it wasn't happening like that at all. Like a play where all the actors had been handed the wrong parts, the lines were garbled and made no sense. To her, the doctor said, "Sit up," and then said to Mrs. Whey, who stood nearby, "While I talk to this one, get Number Ten lined up."

She raised herself first on her elbows, then upright to a sitting position.

"You can put your feet down," he said.

She sat up then, swinging her feet to one side. The table was high and her feet did not touch the floor.

"Too late," the doctor said. "I'm sorry."

"I don't understand."

I don't know how I can make it any plainer. At your stage of pregnancy—I'd say fourteen or fifteen weeks—vacuum aspiration, suction, isn't safe."

Her hands clutched wads of the stiff paper gown that lay across her stomach. Fourteen or fifteen weeks. Silently, her lips formed the words. Fourteen or fifteen weeks was more than three months. "Oh, no," she whispered. "Oh, no!" She could see Bill Lobos's face, with its long dark hair growing from a satanic V on his forehead, as she'd seen it in the darkness, illumined only by the faint light from the dashboard of his car. She could hear Bill Lobos's voice saying, "Take a swallow. A big one. Now another." He had laughed as she had swallowed, choked and swallowed again. "Now, you'll feel better," he said. "And you're going to feel a lot better soon."

Small, dark tadpole shapes were darting in front of her eyes. Had it happened that night, after all?

She slumped at the waist and her head fell forward. The doctor caught her before she could topple from the high table to the floor.

6 / All for Nothing

It was Iris's fault, she told herself. If Iris hadn't made her talk to Bill Lobos the night of the basketball game, she never would have. Nothing would have happened as it did.

Over and over again, she had tried to make herself believe that at least some small part of it was Iris's fault. But it wasn't any use. She knew what she was doing. At least, during the first part of the evening she had known what she was doing.

She had talked to Bill Lobos, left the basketball game with him. She could still remember the way she'd felt picking her way over the feet of a long row of kids, most of whom she knew, aware that Mark Truro was watching her. At the top of the ramp, she had turned to look and saw that he, too, had turned and was staring upward. Even at that distance their eyes had met. Then she had tossed her head and laughed and taking Bill Lobos's arm they had left the gym.

The night was bright and very starry. Walking toward his car, Bill Lobos had put his arm around her waist, under her coat, holding her so tightly that it seemed that her feet scarcely touched the ground.

"I guess we showed *him,* all right," Bill Lobos said. It was strange, she thought, that his thoughts were so much like hers.

He laughed, not as if he were amused, but with a harsh staccato sound. "If there's any one guy in the whole of Cedar City whose guts I really hate, it's Mark Truro. Sometime, I'll tell you why. Tonight, we've more interesting things to do."

He stopped then, in the darkness of the parking area, and pushed her backward against a hood of a nearby car so she could not move. Then he had laid his body against hers and kissed her until she felt as if no breath were left in her body.

He had laughed, this time softly, as she had ineffectually fought against him and then as suddenly he had let go of her. "That's for beginners," he'd said.

She did not know how far they drove before they stopped. He didn't drive like Mark Truro did. Mark drove with his left hand on the wheel, his right hand making a soft gentle closure across her shoulder or placed it lightly on her lap where it rested there with such gentle pressure that she did not miss it until he needed both hands on the steering wheel.

Bill Lobos pulled her so closely to his side that it seemed that a single connecting current held their bodies together. His right hand was placed on the upper, innermost part of her thigh. She did not move away.

When they stopped, it was very dark, the road seeming to end an instant before he doused the headlights of the car. "Pot's for pot-heads. Acid is for the acid-eaters." He laughed softly. " 'Horse' is for the horse-racers—if losing races is your idea of fun. But 'likker is quicker.' I don't know who said that first, but in any case it's for me." He flipped a button on the dashboard of the car, suffusing it with a pale soft light, and brought out a square, squat bottle. "Take a swallow," Bill Lobos was saying. "Take a big one. Now another."

She had swallowed, choked, and swallowed.

"Now you'll feel better," he said. "And you're going to feel a lot better soon."

They had driven on, then stopped again. He raised the bottle to his lips, then passed it to her. She lifted it to her mouth and although she only pretended, or meant to pretend, to drink, she still swallowed enough of the fiery liquid to make her choke. More dribbled down her chin, wetting the front of her dress and coat.

His mouth covered hers, draining her of all vitality. She tried to push him away from her, tried to say "no" but had lost the power to say the simple word.

"Better be moving on again," Bill Lobos said, and started the car.

Bill Lobos didn't live in the woods at all—though she hadn't believed him when he said he did. Fuzzy as her vision was, she could see that the house in front of which they stopped was just an ordinary house in one of the older run-down parts of town. A faint bluish light shone through the slats of crooked Venetian blinds.

Her legs buckled beneath her when she tried to walk and Bill Lobos had finally picked her up and carried her into the house.

There were perhaps a half dozen people in the room. But even if she could have seen clearly through the shifting haze of blue smoke, her mind was too befuddled to count them.

No one looked up. And except for the almost imperceptible movement made as a glowing cigarette was passed among them, no one moved.

"Stoned." Bill Lobos laughed softly. "All of them. But that's what keeps me in business. In any case, they won't bother us. They won't even know what's going on."

The house was small and the air stale and smoky. There wasn't much furniture, either. That much she noticed as she stumbled after Bill Lobos to the kitchen. It was so brightly lighted there that the memory of it was still implanted in her mind like a picture projected in the darkness on a motion picture screen. The sink was full of glasses and dirty dishes. Two skillets on the stove were thick with congealed fat.

He washed out two glasses under the tap, sloshed a couple of inches of dark brown liquid in each, then filled them with a bottle of Coke he found in the refrigerator.

"Drink it."

She shook her head like a child, back and forth. "Don't drink. Never, never drink. Nice girls nev'r, nev'r drink." Then the ridiculousness of it struck her. Even if it was true that before that night the only thing she ever had to drink was some wine at an Italian wedding, she was drinking now, and she'd forgotten or almost forgotten that Mark Truro existed.

She reached for the glass, slopping some more down her front, and tasting it found it was, at least, better than from the bottle. Or maybe it was just because her tongue was numb. The room seemed to be revolving, too. Very slowly. When she looked at Bill Lobos, he had three eyes. One on either side of his nose and another in the middle. It was ridiculous. She sagged against the drainboard of the sink, laughing helplessly.

With the one small part of her mind that seemed to be functioning properly, she thought, "So this is how it feels to be drunk." When Merle, her stepfather, got drunk, he wasn't happy. He stormed through the house cursing and kicking anything that got in his way. When Merle got drunk, afterward he had to "sleep it off." Sometimes, when she came downstairs in the morning she found him half on and half off the davenport, making terrible noises from his mouth and nose.

Remembering, she said, "Go home. Go home, *now.*" Her voice in her own ears sounded thick and unnatural.

"You're crazy," Bill Lobos said. "At first, it was enough for me that you'd been Mark Truro's girl—and what was good enough for him was good enough for me. But now, baby, you turn me on. You really turn me on. And right now, baby, you're not going no place at all." He put down his empty glass and with his three eyes all staring, staring, staring came walking slowly toward her.

"Tired," she said plaintively. "So tired." Yet when she lay down in the darkness beside him and closed her eyes so she could rest a while, the room once again began its strange gyrations. It wasn't revolving gently as it had done before, but was rocking back and forth like the mechanical horse at the supermarket that Precious always had to ride.

Only when he held her tightly, so tightly that there was no room for breath in her body, could she sleep. Once she heard a girl cry out as sharply as if she had been stabbed or was suffering some other grievous hurt.

Someone was shaking her, not too gently. "O.K., sweetheart. Time for beddie-bye." He pulled her dress down and found her shoes.

A soft fine rain was falling. A January rain. It shrouded the street light, casting a pale penumbra outside its shadowed veil, freezing as it fell, tufting the dried spears of grass, the tall awkward weeds, with silver.

"Can you make it?" Bill Lobos asked. "Can you walk, or shall I carry you? I wouldn't want your old man to catch me doing it."

"I can walk." It seemed a matter of pride. She didn't want the Mallards who lived next door—he worked the night shift at the newspaper and his wife waited up for him—seeing her being carried to the door.

He hunted for a long time before he found the key in her purse, then at last she was inside.

The light in the hall upstairs was burning. Merle left that one on so he could check on her. He said he slept with one eye open—when the light went off, he knew she was home—but that was not the truth. Merle slept like a dead man. A noisy dead man.

She turned off the light from the switch in the downstairs hall and, not trusting herself to walk, crawled up the stairs on hands and knees.

She undressed clumsily. A clothes hanger in the closet fell as she was hanging up her dress but Precious, who slept in the next room, did not waken. She put her wet shoes neatly side by side but kicked her panties and pantyhose into the closet. She did not remember putting on her nightgown nor getting into bed.

"I smell throw-up," Precious said. She stood in the doorway of Bonnie Jo's room wrinkling her small, flat nose like a Pekingese. She moved around the room, sniffing, then returned and stood by Bonnie Jo's bed. Her eyes were very blue and protruded slightly. Like Merle's. "I *do* smell throw-up," she said, "and I'm going to tell Mama." She backed away a few feet, then clattered down the stairs. She was wearing her tap-dancing shoes and Bonnie Jo could hear her all the way to the kitchen.

She turned on her side and faced the wall. Her head ached and there was a bitter, metallic taste in her mouth. Drawing her knees up to her chest helped ease a strange, undefinable pain that filled all her lower body.

Her mother opened the bedroom door. "Well, what's wrong now? Merle says unless you're really sick he doesn't want you lying around here all day."

Tears leaked from Bonnie Jo's eyes. She and her mother had never been close, but things were even worse since she married Merle. Now she was always on his side.

"Well?" her mother said again.

"Cramps." Cramps were something her mother understood. Once a month she went to bed for two days and stayed there. Besides, Bonnie Jo felt as if that might really be what was wrong.

"Oh," her mother said. "Well, in that case. If you want the heating pad, it's on the shelf in my closet. On the right-hand side. I won't be here. Merle's dropping Precious off at nursery school and I'm going to a Tupperware party at Hilda's house. Go back to sleep and if the phone rings, don't answer it."

A little later, Bonnie Jo heard her mother tiptoe up the stairs and look in, but she gave no sign that she had heard. Soon after, the car roared out of the drive. Presently she got up, stood at the top of the stairs listening to be sure they were gone.

In the bathroom, she shampooed her hair under the shower, then filled the tub with water as hot as she could stand. She scrubbed herself until her body was pink. She washed her nightgown out by hand but there was nothing to do with her panties and pantyhose but burn them.

This she did, stuffing them into a paper bag and carrying them out to the trash burner in the back yard. The rain which had fallen the night before had frozen into a thick white icy crust, strong enough to bear her weight. Though she'd put on her heaviest coat over her clean nightgown and tied a scarf over her wet hair, she shivered as she stood by the trash burner waiting for the stuff to burn. It did so at last, but not until she had made a trip to the back porch to get dry newspapers to help the blaze along.

She poked at the charred garments until nothing identifiable remained, then went back into the house. There was cold coffee on the stove but even when it was warmed, it was not fit to drink. She poured it in the sink and went back upstairs to her room. Crawling back into bed, she turned her face to the wall and slept.

On her way to school the next morning, she dropped the dress with the "throw-up" on it at the dry cleaner's. It was the last reminder of what she could not remember.

Iris was waiting for her at her locker.

"When I said 'talk to him,'" Iris said indignantly, "I meant 'talk.' Not get up and go *out* with him. Where did you go? What did you do? And why weren't you in school yesterday? Gordy was shocked. He couldn't believe it when you *left*. Honestly." She paused, shifted a load of books from one arm to the other, and gave Bonnie Jo a narrow look as they walked down the hall to class. "I don't know why you're being so secretive. You haven't answered a single thing I asked you."

"You haven't stopped talking," Bonnie Jo said testily. "You haven't given me a chance."

"Well, then . . ."

Bonnie Jo shrugged. "Nothing much. Rode around."

"Is that *all?*"

"Well, we got something to eat. At one of those new places out on River Road." Iris, she supposed would next want to know what they had to eat, so she might as well make up something good. "Steak sandwiches. Beef tenders, you know. French fries. And malts, of course."

"He *would* have money," Iris said, grudgingly. "Gordy says he's a pusher. Sells pot to high school kids all over town and, when he can get it, stronger stuff. If I were you, I'd not have anything more to do with him."

Bonnie Jo's laugh was high-pitched, almost hysterical. "You don't have to worry about *that,*" she said.

Yet after having him hang around and hang around, and after seeing Mark Truro and Sis Claiborne scarcely out of each other's sight, one afternoon after school when Bill Lobos had come by, she'd gone with him in his car.

That time she hadn't been drunk. And she wasn't sorry for him. Still, she half believed that story he'd told her about Mark Truro cheating him out of a free bicycle their first year of junior high. After he had sold 125 tickets to the Boy Scout Jamboree all on his own, Mark Truro had gone out and bought enough extra tickets with his own money to make him the winner.

None of that mattered. She'd just done it. Mostly, she supposed, because only that morning Mark Truro, alone for once, had stopped her in the hall. After so long a time, her nearness to him had made her feel so faint that at first she scarcely understood what he was saying.

"You and I may not be going together anymore, Bonnie Jo," he said, "but I still don't like the idea of you running around with crumb-bums. You know who I mean. For your own sake, I wouldn't like to see you get hurt."

She said, "I'd like to see you drop dead," and had stood there staring at him until he'd flushed and walked away.

Even then, it might never have happened if that same afternoon Sis Claiborne and Mark Truro hadn't been crossing the street to the Sweet Shoppe just as Bill Lobos stopped his car at the corner where she was waiting for the bus.

He'd opened the car door and without saying a word, she'd got in. They'd driven somewhere out in the country and then without even wanting to, much, she'd done it. In broad daylight. In the back seat of his car.

"She's all right," the doctor said. She felt him lift

one of her eyelids and look down at her closely. "She's coming 'round."

The haze was lifting, the room growing brighter. The doctor was smiling, faintly.

"Just how pregnant did *you* think you were?"

"Maybe . . . nine?" The words, which she'd whispered at first, she repeated defiantly. Then was when it had to be. She had known for sure what she was doing.

"When did you have your last period? You must know that?" He was looking at her curiously, but not unkindly.

Tears sprang to her eyes and she shook her head. "I . . . I never know. Sometimes, it's months. Since I first started having them, I never knew."

"That helps explain it," the doctor said, dryly, "but it doesn't alter the facts. The fetus is well developed. Fourteen to fifteen weeks. If you still want an abortion, you'll have to have what is called a "salting-out"—an injection of a salt solution into the uterus. That will trigger a miscarriage some twelve to forty-eight hours later."

Though the words seemed to be coming from very far away, she heard each word distinctly and, strangely, without panic. When she spoke, her voice, though just a whisper was steady. "Well, then, I guess I'll have to have one of those."

7 / Rated "X"

"Come now," said Miss Glynn, popping her head into the cubicle where Bonnie Jo sat hunched in the small straight-backed chair. "It's not that bad. Salting-out's not the end of the world."

Bonnie Jo, in her misery, did not reply. No matter what Miss Glynn said, it *was* that bad. The doctor had put it to her straight. The salting-out process, though basically simple, was also potentially dangerous. When the New York Board of Health had made office salting-outs illegal, they stopped performing them at the clinic and had broken up their equipment. The only way she could have one now, he said, was to find a doctor who would give her the injection in a hospital where she would remain until the abortion was complete. He couldn't do it, because he had no hospital connections. Even if he could, the situation was very tight. Some hospitals allowed no salting-outs on their premises. One that allowed three a day had a waiting list six weeks long. The same thing, he feared, was true in all the other hospitals in the city.

That wasn't all. In a hospital, a salting-out procedure was going to cost considerably more than she had expected to pay for a simple abortion. Even the words "salting-out" were ugly and terrible. Worse than "abortion." She could not bear them. She began to cry, softly, almost noiselessly.

"None of *that.*" Miss Glynn produced a man-sized Kleenex and said "Blow," like a mother to a child. "Now, come with me down to my office where we can talk. I've been having a small conference with some of the rest of the staff, to see what we can do for you."

Bonnie Jo blew her nose and wiped her eyes.

"It's not a good policy for the other girls to see anyone crying," Miss Glynn said as they left the elevator and then waited a moment to be sure that Bonnie Jo actually had stopped crying before they crossed the reception room to her office.

"The first thing," she said practically, "is that you have a place to stay until you can make further arrangements. I've already taken care of that. We've found a room for you in the West Fifties. The woman who runs the place will understand. We've sent several other girls there in the last few months.

"I suggest you go over there right now, leave your things, then get busy on the telephone. Your best bet is to find a doctor outside the city. Outside the city, you won't have to wait so long to get a room in a hospital. Dr. Ochre suggests you first try to get in touch with a man he knows in Syracuse. I've written his name down here. And if he can't help you," she flipped open a copy of a magazine and put it down in front of Bonnie Jo, "there are a lot of good suggestions here. A dozen at least. Follow them all up. If the person you call can't help you, ask them if they know of someone who can.

You can take the magazine with you. It will all work out. You'll see."

Tears swimming in her eyes, Bonnie Jo stared unseeingly at the magazine.

Miss Glynn got up and stood behind Bonnie Jo's chair. "I don't want to hurry you away, but there *are* other girls waiting . . ."

Bonnie Jo stumbled to her feet. "Oh . . . oh . . . I'm sorry."

"And I'm afraid that tomorrow, too, is going to be a very busy day. Saturday, you know. Girls come from all over. But we'll try to keep in touch. You let us know how you come out."

"Oh, yes." Walking and talking in a dream, she had almost reached the door when Miss Glynn stopped her. "Here's the address of your rooming house. I've drawn you a little map to show you how to get there." She pointed with a pencil at a sheet of yellow paper. "Turn left at our front entrance and keep going until you come to the Avenue of the Americas. Then turn left again and you get here." She pointed with her pencil on the map. "One more left-hand turn and you're almost there. The third brownstone on the left-hand side of the street. Do you understand?"

Bonnie Jo nodded, though she really did not comprehend. All that was really important was not to lose the map, never turn right, and keep on walking.

There was a large white cat with yellow eyes sitting in the window of the brownstone house, along with a "Room for Rent" sign. "Only Respectable Clientele Need Apply."

The cat inspected her, narrowing his yellow eyes and flicking his last quarter inch of tail.

Bonnie Jo looked at him, too weary to climb the flight of a dozen or more steps that led to the front door. Miss Glynn had not told her how long a walk it would be. The crosstown blocks she had walked had seemed to stretch forever.

Now that she'd reached the rooming house, she wondered if coming there had been the right thing to do. Her father had said that if she had to spend the night in New York, she should go to the YW. Instead, she had let Miss Glynn take over.

Sitting huddled on the bottom step, she watched the street in front of her strangling in the throes of the late afternoon traffic. Delivery trucks, vans, cars, and taxis all headed the same direction were wedged together in impossible angles seemingly going nowhere. Horns were honked, drivers swore, and intrepid pedestrians wormed their way through the crevices that separated bumper from bumper.

The sidewalk was only a little better. Mesmerized, Bonnie Jo watched as people shoved and jostled their way around a yawning hole in the pavement into which two men were taking turns tossing large wooden crates. Homebound workers darted in delicatessens, bakeries, or liquor stores and emerged, eyes intent and expressions grim. But five o'clock in New York was only four o'clock in Cedar City. Two hours must pass before she could call her father.

She slept scarcely at all. Although the small room to which the white cat and a dour-looking woman wearing a pink housecoat conducted her was on the third floor rear of the brownstone building, even in her semiconsciousness she was aware of the dull roar of traffic, the thin wail of fire engine or ambulance. In one of her fragmentary dreams, Dr. Ochre's face rose up before her. "Well-developed fetus," he was saying. "Fetus . . . fetus . . . fetus." The word was echoed and reechoed as if spoken in a cave of a mountain on the moon. In another dream, she heard her father cry out her name. She awoke and her pillow was wet.

Her telephone call to him had been disastrous. Mrs. Netsch, the landlady, had stood beside her in the hall to be certain she asked the operator to place the call "collect." But even after that, she had not gone away. She had heard everything, from Bonnie Jo's tearful explanation of why she would not be home that night to the search that must be made the next day for a doctor who would perform the more serious and costly operation in a hospital.

The connection had been poor and she had had to repeat almost everything she said. Even with the crackling on the line she could tell her father, too, was close to tears.

"Maybe it would be better," he said, "if you just

came home. Somehow, some way, we'd work something out."

"I can't. I'm here," she whimpered. "I'm going to stay."

"You'll need more money . . ."

"Yes . . ."

"How much more? Bonnie Jo, do you hear me? How much more money will you need?"

She had begun to cry again. "Daddy, I don't know. I'll call you as soon as I find out . . . good-bye."

"Bonnie Jo, don't hang up . . ."

"I'll call you tomorrow night. I promise. . . ."

He was still speaking, saying something, when she hung up the receiver.

Mrs. Netsch stepped forward out of the shadows. "Don't think because I let you use the phone tonight, that you can use it any time you want. Just because you called collect, doesn't mean it won't be put on my bill. And I don't want you tying up the line tomorrow with local calls, either. There are pay phones by the dozen right here in this block." Then she had wrapped her dirty pink robe more tightly about her and, with the white cat sitting close beside her, watched as Bonnie Jo slowly climbed the stairs to her room.

Although she had had nothing to eat the day before, except a cup of coffee and a sweet roll the nurse at the clinic had forced upon her, she still was not hungry.

But she could not go another day on an empty

stomach. She peered through the window of a lunchroom she passed a block or two away from the rooming
house. There were no booths, only a long counter and
a row of high stools. Although it was only a little after
eight o'clock, all were occupied, and behind at least a
half dozen of the diners, another person stood waiting.

In the next few blocks she passed several similar
places, all equally busy. Did no one in New York eat
breakfast at home? She even passed people on the
street carrying cartons of hot coffee and sweet rolls
back to office workers who could not get out to fend for
themselves.

Feeling lightheaded and a little sick, she entered
the next luncheonette she came to. Again, all the stools
were occupied. One man, however, seemed to have
finished his breakfast and was lighting a cigarette to go
with a second cup of coffee. Seeing her reflected in the
mirror behind the counter, he turned and in a moment
had slid off his stool.

"Take my place," he said. "You look as if you'd
just about had it." He slipped a quarter under the edge
of his empty plate and without even seeming to address
her said, "Stranger in New York?"

Eyes brimming, she nodded.

"It's none of my business what you're doing here,
but in New York many are called and few are chosen.
To coin a phrase. If I were in your place, I'd just go
home."

"Friend o' yours?" As Bonnie Jo sat down, a waitress with blond hair done up in a net pulled down to

her eyebrows had started removing the dirty dishes with one hand while she wiped up the counter with the other.

Bonnie Jo shook her head.

The waitress nodded wisely. "I thought as much. And in that case, I won't be hurting your feelings if I tell you I think he's some kind of a nut. Butting in like that. New York is full of nuts. But that's not New York's fault. There's nothing wrong with *New York.* It's the people." She gave the counter a final swipe. "Now that's settled, what are you going to have?"

Bonnie Jo stared at the menu, trying not to look at it too long.

"Orange juice? Coffee? A . . . a toasted English muffin." she said, at last. Everything was so expensive. Even the little she'd ordered would cost more than a dollar. At the Sweet Shoppe, the little eating place across from Central High, you could get the same thing for eighty-five cents.

The orange juice, which came out of a huge vat on the counter, didn't taste right, but she drank it anyway. The English muffin, however, was hot and as Bonnie had observed, had been rather lavishly spread with butter by the waitress in the hair net.

She also observed a phone back at the rear of the lunchroom, next to the kitchen.

After slipping a dime beneath the edge of her plate, she paid her bill at the cashier's cage and received a dirty look along with the five dollars in change that she asked for.

The phone booth, with the door closed, was stifling. However, with the door opened, the smell of hot fat and a ripe spaghetti sauce, already simmering for the lunch trade, made that choice impossible.

Too nervous to read carefully the instructions for making long distance calls from a coin-operated phone, her first two attempts to reach the number of the doctor in Syracuse failed. The third time, however, she talked first to the office receptionist, then to a nurse who, sounding nice, said the doctor was no longer performing salting-outs in any hospital, but named a physician in Ithaca who did.

That call went through more easily. However, the nurse to whom Bonnie Jo spoke said the doctor there was performing salting-outs in several Ithaca hospitals, but that he could not schedule her until he had examined her. Also friendly, she added, "If you're calling from New York, bear in mind that Ithaca is a good five hours' drive and that once you're here, there's no assurance the doctor can schedule you in less than ten days to two weeks."

Bonnie Jo said "Thank you," and hung up. For the past few minutes, a stout man wearing a Nehru jacket and a turban had been pacing back and forth like a sentry in front of the phone booth.

She gathered up her possessions and left. She had spent more than forty minutes' time and over two dollars in toll fees for nothing.

Still, she had no choice but to continue trying. By a quarter after one, she had made calls from a dozen different phone booths. Of those completed, each one had been more discouraging than the one before.

An abortion referral agency, whose number Bonnie Jo had got from an ad in the magazine Miss Glynn had given her, suggested a doctor in Long Island who would perform the operation for three hundred dollars, plus hospital fees. A call to that office, however, revealed the doctor was on vacation. A Clergy and Lay Advisory Service, whose number was also listed in the magazine, said they didn't do "referrals," but when Bonnie Jo began to cry on the phone, she was given the name of a physician in Westchester who might help her.

Crying, however, did her no good when talking to the doctor's nurse. He, she said, was "completely overbooked and overworked," then added the reason. He only charged seventy-five dollars and tried to keep hospital fees to the minimum. Which made the call just that much worse.

Out on the street again, Bonnie Jo felt that she could go no farther. Yet, unless she bought something to eat—and the very thought of food was distasteful—there was nowhere she could even sit down. She leaned with her back against a building to avoid the pedestrian traffic that swirled about her. She did not know for sure where she was, nor how many blocks she had walked since she had left her rooming house that morning.

Keeping close to the wall of the building, she moved slowly down the street. Had she been watching where she was going, she would not have bumped into the large cardboard cutout of a girl outside the movie theater. "Rated 'X,'" a signboard on one side informed her. "Hysterically Funny, Spend Ninety Minutes of Sex-Mad Love and Laughter with Marina Moroni in *Marriage on Monday*," declared a sign that flanked it on the other side.

Bonnie Jo looked at the girl in the box office, chewing gum and filing her nails, then at the price of admission. What "Rated 'X'" in New York City meant, as far as age level went, she did not know. But two dollars and a half did seem a lot to pay for a movie in the afternoon. Still, it was not too much to pay to sit down quietly for a while. She needn't stay, she wouldn't stay —even if it were good—for the whole ninety minutes. A half an hour would be enough. There would be a clean rest room, too. The public restroom she had used the last time had been so filthy it had made her sick.

Inside the theater it was cool and dark and the seat she selected in the middle of a row toward the back was so comfortable that she let out a small, whimpering sigh as she sank into it.

She never knew what *Marriage on Monday* was about. When she woke up, it was intermission. The red velvet curtain covering the movie screen had been drawn and spirited music was issuing from hidden loudspeakers.

A few newcomers were trickling in and choosing seats. All of the old audience seemed to have departed.

She reached for her purse and, not finding it, experienced almost complete panic until she discovered that it had slipped from her lap and was lying on the floor under the seat in front of her. She groveled for it and, half-falling over still downturned seats, reached the lobby.

An usher of whom she asked the time flicked back a French cuff to look at his watch. "Four forty-seven."

She stood there, feeling the energy that had been restored by sleep ebbing away with the knowledge that she had let the rest of the afternoon go by without finding a doctor who would help her.

"Is there a rest room?" Her voice faltered as she asked the question.

"To your right, miss, and down the first flight of stairs."

She splashed water on her face and washed her hands, but there were no towels. Using yards of toilet paper, she dried them. In a corner of the outer room, however, she saw a pay phone.

Scraping together a little pile of coins from her purse, she stacked them before her. Afterward, she was never quite sure whose number it was that she dialed. When an answer came—she had not really expected one so late in the afternoon—she repeated the little speech, spoken so often that it issued forth without conscious thought and ended with a sob. Instead of the answer that invariably came, someone said as practically as if she knew the answer, "You're from out of state? And the pregnancy is well advanced?"

She must have said "Yes," for then the voice replied, "Give me your name and the telephone number at which you can be reached. We will be in touch with you as soon as possible."

Scrabbling through her purse, it seemed to take forever before she found the map Miss Glynn had drawn and the address and telephone number of Mrs. Netsch.

But the voice was still there. Comfortingly, it repeated the information she had supplied, then added with a little laugh, "But don't hold your breath. It will be Monday morning sometime, at the earliest, before we call you."

When the connection was broken, Bonnie Jo sank down into the nearest chair. High-backed, ornately carved, upholstered in red velvet like some preposterous throne, it encompassed her as she sat, arms wrapped in strangling tightness about her waist, and waited for the time to come when she could stop crying.

8 / Subway to Brooklyn

A little after two o'clock the following Monday, Bonnie Jo stood outside the office of a physician in Brooklyn. A brass plate, with the words "Dr. Otto Blaubeuren, M.D.," was fastened to the heavy walnut door.

The call for which Bonnie Jo had been waiting came just at noon, and she had started out soon after. Although Mrs. Netsch had told her exactly how to get there, in her nervousness she had not listened carefully enough and the trip by subway, which should have been simple enough, had turned out to be a nightmare. She had got off one station too soon, then in the cavernous underground had waited in the wrong place for another train to come along.

A tiny black girl with a huge Afro hairdo, to whom she finally appealed for help, got her on the right train and told her where to get off. She had finally emerged, up the littered subway stairs, into a street scene as chaotic as the one she had left more than an hour earlier. She had not known that Brooklyn was another New York, that there would be the same snarling traffic, the almost overpowering fumes of gasoline engines, and the crowds on the sidewalk moving in the same peculiar intricate fashion.

The thought of finding her way to the doctor's office—the address was written on a scrap of paper in her purse—either by walking or public transportation was unthinkable. No matter how expensive it might be, she decided to take a taxi.

But even that was not simple. Although she stood near the curbing, holding up a hand the way she saw other people doing, the taxis that came along were either occupied or their drivers' minds and eyes were elsewhere. She walked another block, then stood again with a timid hand upraised before a cab finally wheeled in sharply to the curb.

She had the address in her hand, but when she gave it to the driver, he turned, scowling. "You can get there on foot faster than I can get you there."

"That's all right." Already she had climbed in the cab and put her head on the back of the seat.

Shrugging, he turned back to the wheel. "You're paying the fare," he said, "not me."

Still, when he stopped the cab he said, "I can't make a left-hand turn here. But if you cross the street you'll find the number you want two or three doors down." She read the meter, added twenty cents to the total and again on the street waited for the light to change before crossing with a tide of people that broke and dispersed like a giant wave on the opposite beach.

The office building for whose number she was looking rose in a great granite cube. The lobby, itself, was as busy as the main street in Cedar City. Her eyes blurred as she studied the alphabetical list of tenants that covered an entire wall between two banks of elevators.

Herded into a musical cage, she was borne upward so swiftly that her stomach seemed left behind. Spewed out on the eighteenth floor, she went down two different corridors before she found the number for which she was looking.

She pushed open the door.

The reception room was larger than she had expected it to be. In it were at least a dozen women, several with young children.

She made her way across a thick-piled carpet to a counter of dark polished wood behind which three women in white uniforms were busy with huge filing cases and ringing telephones. It was several minutes before one of them, a small woman with a sharp face and dark eyes, turned around.

I'm Bonnie Jo Jackson." Her name, when she began to speak came out at first too loud and ended as a whisper. "I . . . someone called me. She said that I . . . I should come here . . . that the doctor . . ." It seemed that only a moment before the room had been abuzz with women's voices and children's chatter. Now there was silence.

"Bonnie Jo Jackson," the woman said loudly. She ran her finger down a list of names and gave Bonnie Jo a quick, inspective look. "Oh," she said. "Oh, yes. The woman from . . ."—mercifully, for a moment, she allowed her voice to trail away—"called me about you," then zeroed in again, loud enough for anyone listening to hear. "But you're going to have to wait. All the women here are Doctor's regular patients. They have appointments. So I'm afraid you're going to have to wait." In midstream, her voice had changed again so that it was almost human.

"I . . . I don't mind waiting."

"You have an address?" The unpleasant nuance had returned.

Bonnie Jo repeated her address at Mrs. Netsch's.

"It may be a rather long time. You understand that."

Bonnie Jo nodded and, turning, looked around the large room. At first glance, all the chairs, all the places on small settees or larger sofas appeared to have been taken. As she stood there, an inner office door opened and a woman who appeared to be older than most of the others in the room emerged. She was smiling broadly. "The doctor says that the next time he sees me he hopes that it will be at the hospital," she told one of the women at the desk. "Everything is fine. Just fine."

As she left, the name of another patient was called out, and Bonnie Jo moved across the room to take the recently vacated portion of a sofa.

One of the occupants, in an attempt to make more room, tried pulling herself together as Bonnie approached, then laughed. "It's not much use, I'm afraid. There's just so much of me. And there's going to be quite a bit more of me before the next two months are over."

Bonnie Jo glanced shyly at her neighbor. She was

young and though not terribly pretty, had a merry look about her.

"When's your baby due?" she asked. "Not for a long time, I'd say, from the looks of you."

Bonnie Jo's hands tightened on the strap of her purse. "I don't know." It was the best she could do.

The girl nodded wisely. "I see. It's your first visit. Well, the time passes faster than you ever think it will, though everybody says the last month is an awful drag. Though not for everybody. You saw that woman who left here just a few minutes ago? The one who said the next time the doctor saw her it would be in the hospital? Her name is Mrs. Crenshaw, and she hasn't minded it a bit. I've talked to her a couple of times since I've been coming. You wouldn't believe it to look at her, but she's forty-two and after being married for almost twenty years is having her first baby. She and her husband, she told me, had given up long ago. Then whammy! Both of them are thrilled to death."

Bonnie Jo prayed silently. If the girl didn't stop talking, she was going to scream.

Prayer didn't do it. The girl went rattling on. "As for Bob and me, well! The minute I stopped taking the pill I was pregnant. I just hope you're as happy . . ." her voice faltered, then she struggled on. "I . . . just hope you're as happy as we are."

Too late, Bonnie Jo had realized that the girl was looking at her ringless fingers. But there was nothing she could do with them now, except grip the handle of her purse tighter still.

A deep red flush had diffused the girl's face. "You're not . . . I'm sorry . . . until now, I didn't notice . . . though not everybody does, since Women's Lib, get married, I mean."

"Mrs. Grolier," said one of the women in white, looking around the room.

In relief at hearing her name called, the girl leaped to her feet and a minute later had disappeared behind the inner door a nurse was holding open for her.

Iris had wanted her to get a wedding ring at the dime store. "For appearances," she had said. "Somehow, it doesn't make it seem so terrible if people think you're married."

Bonnie Jo had refused, even when Iris had offered to go and buy it for her. "If you're going to do it, you're going to do it," she said. "It doesn't make any difference what people think."

Now, she was beginning to think that perhaps Iris had been right. If she'd been wearing a wedding ring, she would not only have been spared the conversation that had just taken place but the one with the woman in the purple pants suit, as well. On the other hand, she wouldn't have got acquainted with Joel Partridge on the plane. She'd scarcely had time to think about him since she'd arrived, but just knowing that he was in New York and that he liked her helped a lot. When it was all over she was going to call him before leaving for home, and who could tell what might happen after that? But not right now, while ugliness was piled on ugliness. Even her little walk in Central Park the day before had been a disaster.

It was Mrs. Netsch, wearing her Sunday wrapper of mint green and fuschia, who made her get out of her room.

"Go for a walk." She'd been peremptory. "Take a ride on a Fifth Avenue bus. Sit on a bench in Central Park. Do anything, except sit humped up in your room all day Sunday. You're enough to give a body the creeps. No one is going to call you before tomorrow morning. That woman told you so, herself."

Although she sounded cross, the mug of hot coffee and two pieces of limp toast she'd carried up to Bonnie Jo's room had helped give her the energy to overcome her revulsion at the yellow-stained and not-too-clean bathtub down the hall and take a bath.

At least, it had been nice outside, and Central Park, which she'd found without too much trouble, was swarming with people.

That was the irony. Why, with all those people, should she have chosen the bench with the crying girl?

Perhaps because crying came so naturally to her now, a little time elapsed before she realized that the small, stifled sobs she heard were not her own but came from the girl who shared the park bench upon which she sat.

The girl could, almost, have been her twin. Her hair, though a little darker, was worn the same way. Her poncho was knitted in shades of rose and pink instead of the one of different blues that she was wearing.

But it was her helplessness, her hopelessness, that made Bonnie Jo, without thinking, reach across the little space that separated them and gently touch her arm. "Is there anything I can do?"

God in Heaven, why had she done it? And why should the words—almost as if Iris had been there to think them for her—have sprung to her mind? Who was she to help anybody? But the damage was done. Like a small opening in a mighty dam, growing larger as the increasing flood of water poured through, the girl began to talk.

Discovering she was pregnant, she had come with her husband and brother to New York from her home outside Boston. There, it had taken them two weeks to collect the three hundred dollars—the amount the abortion referral service she'd been in touch with had said she'd need—plus forty-three dollars for incidentals and a little more for their return trip to Boston.

In New York, however, it had turned out the three hundred dollars referred to the doctor's fee alone, and that the hospital would cost another two hundred seventy-five dollars.

She turned a tear-stained face to Bonnie Jo. "Leaving the doctor's office, I'd already cried so much I couldn't see the buildings. We sold our bus tickets. Called everyone we knew, but we couldn't raise any more money. That night we stayed here, in Central Park."

Bonnie Jo looked away.

"The next morning, we saw some blood banks on Fortieth Street and we each got ten dollars for a pint of blood. Further along the block there was another blood bank. I was too dizzy to give anymore but Ted and Bud did and each of them got ten dollars. All we'd had to eat was a hot dog. Even so, I still kept throwing up. Then the three of us tried to beg, but we were too ashamed and we spent that night in Tompkins Square."

Bonnie Jo got to her feet. She could bear no more. Everything was going to cost more than she had ever thought it would. When she'd talked to her father the night before and he'd asked her how much more money she was going to need, all she could say was that she didn't know.

His voice had crackled with worry and impatience. "You ought to have some idea how much the doctor is going to charge and how much your hospital bill will be. I'm having trouble borrowing. My . . . my credit isn't what it used to be. I don't want to go to a loan shark unless I have to. I don't want to borrow more than you're going to need. Bonnie Jo, are you listening to me?"

"I'm listening," she whimpered, then her voice turned sharp. Her nerves were fraying, too. "Tomorrow, I'm going to see a doctor, maybe. Then I will find out."

Still, he had not been satisfied.

Two hundred dollars more, she'd said, at last.

But if the doctor was going to charge three hundred dollars! And if the hospital would cost almost three hundred more, she would soon be crying on a bench in Central Park like the girl who sat beside her. Sharp little sobs were now punctuating her words. "Last night my husband was so desperate he walked along St. Mark's Place trying to solicit a . . ."

She had not waited to hear the rest. She had simply walked away. Without looking back she had walked away, knowing that the girl's bewildered tear-filled eyes were following her.

So now, deep as her own problems were, fresh guilt lay upon her. At least, she could have *listened*. Wrapped in her cocoon of self-pity, she was scarcely listening when the nurse called her name. Startled, she looked about her. Everyone had gone.

She got up and started across the room where the sharp-faced woman in white, with an impatient look, was holding open the inner office door.

Bonnie Jo, who was sitting in the chair the nurse had indicated when the doctor entered, raised her eyes to his face then as quickly looked away for fear that in a moment of hysteria and weakness she might laugh.

Had Dr. Blaubeuren been wearing a forest ranger's hat and uniform instead of a neat dark suit, he would have born an even more striking resemblance to Smokey the Bear.

"You find your situation amusing?" The doctor's voice was a soft, deep growl.

Before he'd finished speaking, she was whimpering.

"No. no. Of course not. You are not amused. You are tired and I am tired. I was at the hospital at two thirty this morning to deliver one mother and was there again a little before six to deliver another woman." He was smiling a little. "That is correct usage, you know. Sometimes, even physicians are lax and talk about 'delivering a baby,' as if it were a package. And you, I expect, have not slept much either, the last few . . . how many is it . . . weeks?"

"Fourteen or fifteen, the other doctor said. Though I . . . I didn't think it was so much."

"That happens, too. Women do not know. They think this. They think that. Many times they are wrong."

The doctor got up, moving slowly almost clumsily around the desk, carefully selected a pipe from a rack that held a dozen or more, then as carefully returned it to its niche. "We all have our desires, our needs. Your needs and desires are not mine, nor mine yours. I and my wife of forty years have never had a child of our own. I find my chief joy in bringing wanted babies into the world. Yet, we must all help each other when we can. So, although the law says that physicians in this state have the power, legally, to destroy, I must have my own reasons before I can consent." He sat down, heavily, leaned forward, elbows upon the cluttered desk. "So now you, if you will, please, begin at the beginning and tell me how you got into this predicament, we will see what can be done."

9 / Letter of Consent

There was nothing for her to do, Dr. Blaubeuren said, but wait until a hospital bed became available.

It might be only a day. But again, it might be a week.

In the early spring dusk, she made her way back to Mrs. Netsch's. At that hour the press of people was even greater than before. They seemed to pour from the mouths of buildings, buses, and subway stairs; to mass themselves in a solid phalanx on the wide sidewalks.

A week! She could not endure a week of waiting. Nor could she afford it. Each day that passed she owed Mrs. Netsch more money. That, plus what she ate—little as it was—taxi, bus and subway fares, a new pair of pantyhose, as well as all the other little things—Kleenex, a bottle of detergent—all added up. That night when she counted the money in her purse she found that already she had spent more than forty of the two hundred dollars she had brought with her.

But the money spent was only the beginning. The hospital, Dr. Blaubeuren said, would demand an advance cash payment of $325.00. That was even more than the crying girl's hospital charged. It didn't help much to learn that it covered everything. Medication, delivery room, anaesthetic. *Anaesthetic.* Until the doctor had told her otherwise, she had thought she would have a general anaesthetic. That wouldn't be so bad because she would be put to sleep and not know what was going on. But general anaesthetics weren't given with salting-outs. Only the local kind. With a local anaesthetic she would know all the time what was going on. Always she would remember.

If Dr. Blaubeuren had not told her he would accept his $350.00 fee in installments, with a down payment of only $75.00, she could not have brought herself to tell her father how much the whole thing was going to cost.

A long silence had followed, then "You . . . you're sure you don't want to come home?"

"Not now. I . . . I've gone through too much. Maybe the doctor will call saying I can go to the hospital tomorrow."

"I'll see what I can do."

For most of the next thirty-six hours, she slept. Once during that time Mrs. Netsch brought her a pot of tea and a sardine sandwich, most of which she fed to the white cat who, since the first day, had inexplicably become her friend. Another time, she brought a bowl of soup called borscht, which was made of beets and, equally inexplicable, was delicious.

The call from Dr. Blaubeuren's office came about noon on Wednesday, and gave her the address of a hospital in Brooklyn where she was to be not later than three o'clock that afternoon.

Fortunately, the morning's mail brought a bank

draft for three hundred dollars from her father. She cried as she read the little note that accompanied it. "I hope this will take care of everything O.K., except for the rest of the doctor's bill. I wish there was some other way to help. If your mother and I had done different, maybe all this wouldn't have happened. Somehow, I will try to make it up to you. Love, Dad."

On her way to the subway, Bonnie Jo passed a shop with pretty nightgowns and bra-slips in the window and on sudden impulse went inside. For $7.95 plus tax, she bought a dainty pink nylon nightgown trimmed with lace, a pair of white panties with "I love you" embroidered on them in blue, and a little Japanese kimono.

The clerk smiled as she wrapped the purchases in tissue paper. "For your trousseau?"

Bonnie Jo shook her head. All she knew was that she did not plan to wear the nightgown in the hospital. Maybe she would save it until she really did get married. Maybe to Joel Partridge?

Twice, in the last two days, she had dreamed about him. Both times the happy dreams—she could remember nothing of them except they were walking together in a meadow—had crowded out ones of nightmare proportions.

The clerk smiled as she handed Bonnie Jo the paper sack with nightgown, kimono, and panties inside. "Have a nice day," she said.

Coming out of the subway, she hailed a cab as she

had done before, only with more difficulty. The trip also was longer. At times, traffic did not move at all. A cold spring rain had begun to fall. Umbrellas sprang up like varicolored mushrooms and in such profusion that the sidewalks seemed roofed with them.

When the taxi drew into the curbing before a huge cube of dirty gray stone, Bonnie Jo peered out uncertainly. "Are you sure this is it?"

"It ain't Park Avenue, sister," the driver said. "But my kid had his appendix out here—it had ruptured even—and he survived it." He punched a change holder on the dashboard. "What are you in for?"

"It's not me. I . . . I'm going to visit a friend."

"My mistake. Seeing the little suitcase, and you not looking too good, if you don't mind my saying so, I thought maybe you was going to have one of them abortions."

Without replying, she took the change from the five-dollar bill she had given the driver.

"No offense, miss."

"That's all right." Strangely, it *was* all right. It no longer mattered what anyone said. It was as if all her feelings had been blunted, hammered out of shape, perhaps even destroyed, since she'd been in New York.

The cold rain beat down on her long fair hair as she walked toward the hospital entrance. It soaked through the soles of her sandals that were already wearing thin after miles of walking and wet the sack that held the pink nightgown and the panties that said "I love you."

She didn't mind. Although the rain was cold, it

was cleansing. Soon it would all be over. Soon she would be going home and life could begin again.

Inside, the hospital wasn't like any of those in Cedar City. Not that she'd ever been a patient in any of them, but she had visited people there. In Cedar City, even St. Agnes Hospital, which hadn't moved into its new building yet, was nice. There, the nursing sisters still wore white habits—at least, the old ones—and floated down the corridors as if they were rolling along on invisible wheels. And on every floor, there was a statue of Mary, all blue and white, with flowers in front of it and a place to kneel down and pray.

The lobby of this hospital looked like a bus station. All the chairs were filled with men and women and a scattering of children, most of whom were eating sandwiches, potato chips, and candy bars.

A feeling of nausea that she'd experienced earlier in the day rose within her, and a little film of darkness passed in front of her eyes and she began to shiver with cold.

"Are you all right?"

The voice at her side was soft, faintly accented, but the arm slipped around her waist was strong and supportive.

"I . . . I don't know."

The woman who had appeared at her side, however, was old. Her skin was crisscrossed with a thousand tiny crinkles, like tissue paper that has been crumpled, then smoothed out again. She was wearing a turquoise smock with a little insignia on the pocket.

"Are you coming to see someone here, or perhaps it is you who is the patient?"

"... The patient."

"Your doctor tells you to come here?"

Bonnie Jo nodded.

"I ask, because otherwise there is no use in coming. Even so, to get admitted sometimes one must wait. We go this way."

As she spoke, she began propelling Bonnie Jo toward an office with a lighted sign above the door that said "Admissions."

"Oh, yes. Forms to fill out, and if you're here for the abortion ... yes? ... you must have money to pay. They trust no one for that. Everyone must pay at the beginning. It is too bad, but it is the rule. Sometimes, those who need do not get. But do not be afraid. I will stay with you until you are safely in your room."

Her heart still pounding, Bonnie Jo lay on her side on the high white hospital bed listening to the rattle and clash of dishes and carts in the hall outside her room. If Mrs. Zeema had not stayed with her, she never would have managed the long process of admittance that included the filling out of another lengthy form, the inspection and finally the acceptance of the bank draft her father had sent.

Since then, when Mrs. Zeema had turned her over to a nurse wearing a cap with a black band on it who had instructed her to undress, hang her clothes in the closet, and put on a stiff white nightgown she found on the bed, there had been a steady parade of people in and out.

First, a girl in a white uniform, carrying a tray of little bottles. "We need a sample," she said, and without any more conversation felt for the blue vein on the inside of Bonnie Jo's elbow and after two false tries succeeded in extracting a cylinder of purplish blood. She then pressed a dab of cotton on the puncture and saying "Press and hold," departed.

Another nurse, not yet capped, took her down the hall to leave a urine sample.

The rattle of dishes in the hallway was growing louder and the lovely smell of stewed chicken filtered into the room. For the first time in days, she was ravenously hungry. She sat up and drew back the curtains at the foot of the bed and looked around the room. The bed opposite hers was still unoccupied, as it had been when she arrived. The curtains around the other two beds, however, had been drawn back completely and for the first time she could see the women sharing the room.

A moment later, a tall thin young man wearing a white jacket entered. He was carrying a tray which he presented to the prettier of the two women. Her bed jacket was pink and her heavy dark hair which hung in a single plump, glossy braid over one shoulder was tied with a pink ribbon.

"Soup, chicken, and biscuits, fruit salad, milk, and tea!" she cried when she saw the tray. "George Eliot Sebastian will eat well tonight!"

The young man grinned, went out in the hall and a moment later returned with another tray. However, before he could put it down before the woman in the other bed next to the window, she waved it away. "I'm not nursing," she said. "I don't have to eat their lousy food. My husband's bringing me a sausage and mushroom pizza and my kid is going to drink from a bottle and like it."

The woman in the pink bed jacket went on eating. "I would not *not* nurse George Eliot for anything. Like natural childbirth, it's part of an experience I wouldn't miss."

"Well, I *could* miss it," said the other. "That's just the difference between you and me."

Bonnie Jo withdrew her head from the opening in her green curtain and sat back in bed. When her tray came, she was going to eat in privacy with the curtains shut.

She listened intently for the young man to return, but when he did it was only to remove the tray of the woman in the pink bed jacket. Not until the clatter of dishes and rumbling of carts in the hall had subsided did a nurse appear. Young, cheerful and pink-cheeked. She took a chart that Bonnie Jo did not even know was there from the foot of the bed.

"Let's see," she said. "You're the saline injection, aren't you? Scheduled for tomorrow morning. Is everything all right?"

Bonnie Jo could not keep her voice from trembling. "I . . . I guess. Except I'm hungry."

The pink-cheeked nurse smiled. "Too bad somebody didn't tell you. But if you're a saline injection you get no 'din-din.' It may be an unnecessary precaution, but that's the way we do it around here. Just don't think about being hungry and you'll be all right." A moment later, she was gone.

Bonnie Jo lay back on her pillow and bit hard on her lower lip to keep from crying. In the hallway outside, a telephone rang on and on. A new voice took over the loudspeaker and began calling endlessly for a doctor whose name Bonnie Jo could not make out.

The evening visiting hour was announced by chatter, laughter and a steady clip-clop of footsteps up and down the hall. The woman in the pink bed jacket exclaimed joyfully when her husband arrived, apparently bringing flowers, then their two voices dropped to a whisper.

The other woman's husband arrived soon after. He was a little drunk but he'd remembered to bring the sausage and mushroom pizza and a little later, Bonnie Jo heard the curtain being drawn, and after a little noisy horseplay, all was silent.

A bell signaling the end of the visiting hour jangled noisily, and again amidst a fresh burst of chatter, laughter, and the shuffle of feet in the hall, the two husbands departed.

The baby belonging to the woman in the pink bed jacket was brought in to nurse, was at length taken away, lights were turned off, and the room grew silent.

Outside in the hall, however, a telephone still rang

and the voice on the loudspeaker tried once again to reach the doctor with the unintelligible name.

It must have been hours later that the door opened and the curtain at the foot of her bed parted. "You still awake?" Bonnie Jo could not see the nurse's face but her voice, though brusque, was not unkind. In one hand she held a miniature paper cup. "Sleeping pill," she said. "Doctor's orders. He doesn't want you crying your head off all night long."

Bonnie Jo cupped the pill into the palm of her hand, then took it with a swallow of stale water from the bedside table.

"Get some sleep now. O.K.?"

"O.K."

"And no more crying."

"O.K." She wished she could have seen the nurse's face.

She awoke to the rattle and clatter of dishes and the fragrance of coffee. If she had not been allowed dinner the night before, she would not be given breakfast. But that did not matter now. She waited until the bathroom was free, then washed her face and hands, brushed her teeth and then her hair.

The nurse had said the injection was scheduled for the first thing that morning, and she wanted to be ready. But time was passing. She got up and looked at the clock on the wall above the horseshoe-shaped nurse's station. Nine o'clock. Then ten o'clock, and Dr. Blaubeuren still had not arrived.

The Sebastian baby was brought in to nurse, beds were changed, nurses' aides came and went.

Once a nurse had popped her head inside the green curtain and said, "You don't have to just lie there, you know. Get up and walk around. Go down to the nursery and see the babies. No, I guess you wouldn't want to do that. But in any case, you won't have to wait much longer. Dr. Blaubeuren just phoned to say he'd be in to see you shortly."

The nurse went away, but Bonnie Jo did not get out of bed. Fear seemed to have paralyzed her. Ever since she'd known she was going to have the saline injection, she had wished she knew more about it. Like where it would be given. How long what they called "the procedure" would take. The most horrid conjecture of all was about the needle. Like where it would go. Down through her belly button? That was where mother and baby were attached. Everybody knew that. Everyone had one. A belly button. Except Adam and Eve, of course. Now she was glad she didn't know, well, anything. Dr. Blaubeuren, in his office, had been a lot more concerned about finding out how she got pregnant and when, and if she had the money to pay the hospital, and enough money, finally, to pay *him*, than he had been about explaining what would happen to *her*.

She felt his presence before she saw him. When, halfway between sleeping and waking, she opened her eyes, he was standing beside her bed. He took her hand in his and looked down at it lying there, as small and white as a starfish. His reddish brown eyes were liquid behind his thick glasses.

"I'm sorry to be so late. I've been tied up with the hospital administrators since seven thirty this morning. I . . . I'm afraid I have bad news. They have refused to allow me to give the saline injection because you are a minor. One must be eighteen. Until we have the consent of your parents—in this case, of your father—there is nothing I can do."

"But he *wants* to help me. If he hadn't wanted to help me, he wouldn't have given me the money. You know that . . ."

"*I* know it. The hospital does not."

"They could telephone him. I mean, he could call *them* . . ."

Dr. Blaubeuren shook his head. "It is not that simple. They must have a letter from him, saying it is approved. It must be notarized."

She looked down at her legs, thin now to the point of emaciation, hanging down over the side of the high hospital bed. "But I . . . I can't wait. There isn't time. School. I can't be gone . . . forever. People will know . . ."

Dr. Blaubeuren dropped her hand. "I am sorry. It is not my rule. But it has to be this way. Or . . . not at all."

10 / The Eleventh Day

Never had Bonnie Jo thought she would ever want to go back to Mrs. Netsch's.

But anyplace would have been better than *this* hospital. That was because it really disapproved of abortions and would prefer that none be performed on its premises at all. The nurse with the black band on her cap had told her that. King's County Hospital, she said, would have been the best place to go—that is, if she could have gotten in. There, they had a six-bed abortion unit with four shifts of patients a day. Two shifts of d. and c.'s came in in the morning, salting-outs were at two in the afternoon, and another shift came in at six. The last batch stayed overnight, were awakened early the next morning, given breakfast, and then sent home. The salting-out patients had a special six-bed room all to themselves. Even the nurses who worked there were screened. If they weren't sympathetic toward people having abortions, they didn't work on that floor at all.

How neat that hospital sounded!

In this hospital, you never could tell about the nurses. Some were nice and friendly, while others acted as if you'd just killed somebody. In her room now, instead of just the woman in the pink bed jacket there were *three* nursing mothers, all of whom talked endlessly among themselves about how many ounces of milk they'd given their babies at the last feeding. Big deal, she thought. *Big deal.* Lying on her bed with the green curtains pulled around her, she had no choice but to listen to them going on. Even when her curtains were open they never spoke to her. She told herself she didn't care, but tears seeped from her eyes as she remembered a book she'd had to read for English junior year. *The Scarlet Letter.* Hester . . . what was her name . . . Prynne had been an outcast, too. The book hadn't had much meaning for her then, although Miss Nicholas, the teacher, had tried to start the class thinking about society's attitudes toward things and if they'd changed since then.

When she couldn't stand anymore—visiting hours when the fathers and grandparents came were the worst—she got up and wandered around waiting for the letter from her father to come.

She had called him at his office right after Dr. Blaubeuren had talked to her. The company frowned on the practice of employees being called to the phone during working hours, but she had no other choice. He'd sounded worried when he'd answered. The important thing, though, was that he promised to write the letter, have it notarized and mail it that very day. Air mail special delivery.

She kept going over and over the time it would take before the letter arrived and Dr. Blaubeuren could give her the injection. If her father had taken the letter to the main post office during his lunch hour, it should have gone out that afternoon. In that case, it would already have left Chicago and be on its way to New York. It might even be in New York this very minute waiting to be delivered! Her heart quickened its beat, but not with apprehension. She didn't even worry what the anaesthetic or labor would be like—the women in her room talked a lot about that, too—all she wanted was to get it over with and go home.

Though she'd only been in the hospital a little over twenty-four hours, it already seemed like a week. There was nowhere to go, nothing to do except walk around. She didn't *want* to look in all the open doors, but she did. Although nearly all the rooms had potted plants and vases of flowers sitting around, the private rooms were so filled with them they looked like florists' shops, with the new mother sitting like a queen on her high white bed.

And the nursery. She could scarcely walk anyplace at all on the floor without passing it. And when she did, it exerted such a powerful attraction that she always stopped. Sometimes, she counted the number of little beds lined up row by row, or tried to read the names printed on the card at the head of each. Baby Ginsberg, Baby Olivetti, Baby Sforza, Baby O'Reagen, Baby Schmidt . . . almost every nationality you could think of. It was kind of interesting, too, to see how different the babies were. Before, she'd thought all babies looked alike. But that was wrong. Some were as red and wizened as dried-up apples with thick black hair covering their tiny heads. Others were merely pink and had little or no hair at all. She wondered if the day would ever come when people could look at other people without looking at their differences.

There were other differences, though, that couldn't be seen. Some would have good lives and grow up happy. Others might wish they had never been born. Despite the three women in her room, she knew that not all of the babies in the nursery had parents who wanted them. Some of them, at this very moment, were wishing they had never been born.

It was as close as she could come to making herself believe she was doing the right thing.

She was moving down the hall to the room where the premature babies were kept, each in its own tiny, temperature-controlled capsule, when she heard the commotion in the hall behind her.

"Out of the way, *please*," a voice said sharply.

Bonnie Jo turned to see one of the "preemie" units being rapidly trundled down the hall. The man behind it was still wearing coat, cap, and surgical mask. Two other nurses, also wearing masks, moved swiftly along beside him.

"Will you please go somewhere *else?*" said the nurse who'd spoken first. Almost roughly, she pushed Bonnie Jo to one side as she held open the door to the premature nursery and the doctor, cart, and nurses followed.

Watching from a distance, Bonnie Jo soon after saw another man arrive and the man who'd pushed the cart come out.

132

He took off his cap and wiped his hand across a forehead beaded with sweat. But it wasn't until he took off his mask that she recognized Dr. Blaubeuren.

None of the nurses she asked would tell her what had happened, or whose baby it was. "Later," one said. Another said, "Not now." The nurse with the pink cheeks, who usually was nice, pretended that she had not heard.

It was while she was still picking at the food on her breakfast tray Friday morning that the nurse with the black stripe on her cap came in.

"Sorry," she said, "but I'm going to have to take your tray. You're having your saline injection very soon."

"The letter from my father *came?*"

"No one let me in on the details," the nurse said, removing the tray from Bonnie's reach. "But if the letter was the thing holding up the parade, it must have come. Dr. Blaubeuren has left orders. Someone will be in to prepare you shortly."

A little later, a different nurse brought her a red and white capsule in a small paper cup. Sometime after that, another figure appeared, deftly performed some task, and said, "There is no reason you couldn't walk down the hall for your injection, but we might as well do it in style."

Too drowsy to care, she was rolled onto a cart and trundled rapidly down the hall.

The room was white and very bright. Light shone

133

down from everywhere. Curiously, she was not afraid. Something was placed over her eyes and held there firmly but gently.

She heard the murmur of voices, then there was silence. Someone was holding her hand. Something sharp was inserted in her cervix and she winced. Was it the anaesthetic she had dreaded or the saline injection? She neither knew nor cared. Time seemed to be standing still. When the covering was removed from her eyes she could see that the figures that had been ranged about her had moved back and Dr. Blaubeuren was leaning over.

"In twelve to twenty-four hours your labor will begin. How long after that it will take, we shall have to wait and see."

"Will you be here?"

"Oh, yes. I will be here."

"Thank you," she whispered. "Thank you."

"You'd be a lot better off if you'd get out of bed and walk around," the nurse with the black stripe on her cap said. "You'll know it when something is beginning to happen."

"Will it begin like ... I mean, will it be like cramps?"

"I haven't time to discuss it with you now," the nurse said. "We have two critical cases on the floor demanding our attention."

Bonnie Jo put on her little Japanese robe and slippers and went out in the hall.

134

Something *was* wrong. She could feel it in the air.

There was no one on duty at the nurse's station, which was strange. Usually, there was one person there. The telephone was ringing unanswered and the voice on the loudspeaker called in vain for first one doctor then another. The door to the room next to hers, vacant when she arrived, was now closed and a "No Visitors" sign had been placed upon it.

She went on down the hall to the room next to the nursery. The man in the gray suit and two nurses were standing near the bed she'd seen wheeled into the room the day before.

A moment later, when one of the nurses came out, Bonnie Jo darted forward. "The baby in there—is it one of your critical cases?"

The nurse paused. "Why, yes, he is. Though I don't know what possible difference it could make to you."

"I . . . I just wondered."

"Please do your wondering somewhere other than outside the nursery. We are trying to *save* this infant's life."

Bonnie Jo drew herself close to the wall and like a shadow returned to her room and closed the curtains around her.

When she awoke, the room, except for the small L of light showing through the barely opened door, was dark. The soft sounds of breathing came from the three beds around her. A sharp sudden pain shot across her abdomen and she let out a small involuntary cry. She drew her knees up to her chest and waited until it came again.

The pains were so persistent now that she could not go back to sleep. From far away she heard a church bell toll once, then twice.

She got out of bed and, caught by a sudden pain, sagged against it until she was able to straighten up and walk.

The nursing station was a pool of light surrounded by encroaching shadows. A gray-haired nurse Bonnie Jo had never seen before was leaning over the desk writing.

"I . . . I think it's going to happen. . . ."

The nurse looked first at Bonnie Jo, then at her watch. "According to Dr. Blaubeuren's record, it should be some time yet. I suggest you go down to the lounge area. There's no one there at this hour and you won't be disturbing the mothers in your room. A few exercises might help. Sit-ups, bicycling, jumping up and down. Of course, you wouldn't dream of doing such things if you were having a live baby."

Bonnie Jo crept off down the corridor, past the partially closed doors behind which mothers still slept. But before she could reach the lounge area, the gray-haired nurse had caught up with her.

"I should not have said what I did. It was wrong of me to let my personal feelings show. If Dr. Blaubeuren found out, I'd lose my job. I'd appreciate it if you just forgot . . . what I said."

Bonnie Jo nodded wordlessly.

"When you need me, call."

Tears filled Bonnie Jo's eyes as she stood before the window at the end of the lounge looking out over the city. A pain came and she grimaced, then counted until one came again. Already the first streaks of light that presaged the morning were beginning to show in the sky. On the street below, there was the steady movement of traffic and a few pedestrians, even at this early hour, moved steadfastly forward as they hurried along the sidewalk.

If she were home, she'd still be sleeping. It would be hours yet before she would have to leave for school. Already, she had missed four days. She wondered if Miss Murchison, the girls' advisor, had called her mother. If she had, her mother most likely would have been able to make up a lie about her having the flu or a bad cold that would sound convincing.

She wasn't so sure about Iris. Not that Iris would mean to give anything away, but if any of the kids at school asked Iris where she was, she'd either stammer around and blush or else make up some lie so fantastic that no one would believe it. The next thing, everyone in school would know.

A pain caught her suddenly and she crouched, knees drawn upward to her chest. She shouldn't have told Iris, but neither could she have done without her. Iris was the one who'd thought of calling the crisis center and it was through the crisis center she was able to get her appointment at the abortion clinic in New York.

The hospital had awakened with the city.

Bonnie Jo crept back to her room.

Although the pains were coming with increasing frequency, another six hours were to elapse before a nurse, coming in to check on her, said "Hold tight and I'll call Dr. Blaubeuren. Because of Mrs. Crenshaw, he spent the night in the building."

Again, it was the white, bright room with figures ranging round her. Always she would remember the bright, intent eyes shining in the masked faces. Then her body was swallowed up in pain so intense that it obliterated everything except the voice of Dr. Blaubeuren who, from very far away, was talking to her, cajoling her, telling her what to do.

Suddenly, the pain was gone and her body seemed to have no weight at all. A fragment of a thought floated through her mind. Could she have died . . . gone to heaven? She smiled. No, that wasn't it at all. She just wasn't pregnant anymore.

She lay in her green-curtained niche, her face to the wall, not knowing when night faded into day or day into night.

If, before, no one had paid much attention to her, now people were coming and going all the time. Thermometers were thrust into her mouth, shots administered, sponge baths given, blood samples drawn, ice water forced upon her. Dr. Blaubeuren, in his shaggy bear-brown suit, his eyes red-rimmed and tired, seemed never very far away.

Once, she asked him "Am I going to die?" and he shook his head and, smiling a little, answered, "Not this time."

Late Sunday afternoon when he came, he said, "You're still running a little temperature, but if you can get a seat on the plane tomorrow, I think I'll let you out of here."

When she cried, he patted her hand. "I want a little talk with you, however, before you go."

A nurse's aide went with her when she called the airline for a reservation but turned away when Bonnie Jo, crying, called her father to say she was coming home.

The next morning early, to test herself, she walked down to see the babies. She had thought she might not bear to look at them, but instead they made her smile. The whole room was a sea of tiny red faces and waving arms.

In the intensive care unit next door, however, the crib that had held the "critical case" was no longer there.

The red-cheeked nurse came by as she stood there.

"The baby who was having . . . having such a hard time . . . Did it . . . I mean, did he . . ."

"We all did our best, but it wasn't good enough."

"The baby's mother . . . Mrs. Crenshaw?"

"Being an older woman didn't help, but Dr. Blaubeuren pulled her through." She paused, gave Bonnie Jo a careful look before going on. "The sad thing, it was her first child and she won't be able to try again."

Bonnie Jo averted her face. She had known without asking that the woman in Dr. Blaubeuren's office who'd enjoyed every minute of being pregnant was the baby's mother.

"I'm sorry."

The young nurse's voice was cool, thoughtful but not unsympathetic. "Whose baby it is does make a difference, doesn't it?" she said.

An hour later Bonnie Jo was dressed and her suitcase packed. In addition to what she'd carried in it when she arrived were the Japanese kimono, the pink nightgown, and the panties with "I love you" embroidered on them. In her purse were a prescription for an antibiotic to control her low-grade fever and a month's supply of an oral contraceptive.

She hadn't wanted to take the pills. "It's not going to happen again," she said.

Dr. Blaubeuren smiled. "But it sometimes does— regardless of one's intentions."

"Not to me," she said. "Never."

"Then keep them until you're married." He smiled again. "Most men, even the best of them, expect their wives to take care of contraception."

Two different nurses and one aide asked her if she wanted someone to go with her while she waited for

140

the taxi to take her to the airport. She shook her head. It was almost easier when everyone was not so kind.

On her way to the elevator she passed a young man pushing an empty surgical cart. For the first time since she'd had the abortion, she thought about Joel Partridge. With one small part of her mind she wondered if he had ever got his job as an orderly at a Brooklyn hospital.

But she no longer was worried about its being *this* hospital.

That morning, for the first time in over a week, she had really looked at herself.

Should she and Joel meet in a corridor now, he probably would not recognize her. Leaving New York eleven days after she had arrived, her face seemed to have aged a year for every day she had been there.

J
EYE Eyerly, Jeannette

Bonnie Jo, go home